After being medically discharged from the military, Cian Huntsman finds solace in two things—working out to keep his mobility and online gaming. In one game, he comes across PraernaTheResilient. Cian engages the man. He soon finds himself fascinated by him, and they share many conversations, even outside the game.

Cian soon realizes he wants more from Praerna and asks if they can meet. To his disappointment, Praerna says no, reminding him that he prefers online anonymity due to a disfigurement—hence his name—resilient. Having scars himself, Cian assures Praerna that whatever it is won't matter to him. To Cian's disappointment, Praerna shuts down communication with him.

Unable to let it rest, Cian enlists the help of an army buddy and hacker to aid him in searching for Praerna via his IP address. Once found, he goes there to surprise his friend . . . and maybe get some answers. What he finds is that the paranormal world exists and that Praerna is a gargoyle. Cian learns that his obsession with Praerna is caused by the Fates, as they are mates—the other half of each other's souls.

Can Cian come to grips with his new reality in time to help the gargoyles when his buddy warns him that others in the area are searching for them, too?

The Cyber Huntsman
Copyright © 2023 Charlie Richards
ISBN: 978-1-4874-3888-3
Cover art by Angela Waters

Published by eXtasy Books Inc

Look for us online at:
www.eXtasybooks.com

THE CYBER HUNTSMAN
A PARANORMAL'S LOVE: BOOK
THIRTY-NINE

BY

CHARLIE RICHARDS

DEDICATION

It always seems impossible until it's done.
~Nelson Mandela

CHAPTER ONE

Oh . . . wow! I, uh, I never expected you to ask that.
The words showed up on Cian Huntsman's computer screen, and he watched with bated breath for more . . . for an actual answer to his question. He'd been conversing with a man with the screen handle PraernaTheResilient for nearly six months. A few weeks prior, Cian had shocked himself when he'd realized that his heart raced with anticipation every evening while looking forward to chatting with Praerna.

They'd met on a game they both enjoyed — an adventure game where you completed missions and quests to win bonuses and prizes for your character. After doing a number of missions together, they'd begun chatting about things other than the game. That had led to them moving their dialogue to a chat platform.

Every night, Cian met Praerna to chat, even if the other man didn't have time to play their online game together. He'd learned that Praerna worked nights, so technically, while Cian was winding down for the day, the other man was just starting his. Cian was still a bit uncertain as to what Praerna did, knowing only that he worked at a large, secluded estate and his duties shifted from week to week.

One of the first things Cian had asked was about Praerna's name, why he'd used the term *resilient*. Praerna had explained that the prior management had been strict and harsh. Infractions or mistakes in one's duties had been met with the harshest of punishments.

1

Cian got the impression that, while Praerna hadn't said it, he suspected there had been physical abuse.

When Cian had asked why Praerna hadn't left, his answer had been a little vague, saying only that it was a family position he couldn't get away from. After that, Praerna had quickly assured him that things were different. The people in charge now were kind and encouraging, creating a wonderful environment for everyone at the estate.

Cian sort of wondered if Praerna wasn't part of some kind of religious commune. Except, most of them didn't have the sort of technology his friend seemed to have access to. When Cian had set up his gaming systems, he'd used the best equipment he could get his hands on—some of it almost military grade—and when Cian talked about it, Praerna seemed to know exactly what he was referring to.

So many contradictions with him. So fascinating.

To that end, Cian had finally taken the plunge and had asked if he and Praerna could meet. He wanted to see the guy who made his heart race with anticipation. Once he'd had the idea of asking for a meet-up in real life, Cian hadn't been able to get it out of his head.

It had taken him nearly two weeks to gather the courage.

Except, Praerna still hasn't given me a response.

Frowning at his screen, Cian confirmed that Praerna was still online. He hovered his fingers over the keys, trying to decide what to say. After a few seconds of hesitation, he began typing.

I know that probably came out of left field.

Cian paused and swallowed. He wondered if this was what it felt like to ask someone on a date. Not something Cian had bothered to do since he'd been discharged from the military.

But we've spent so much time talking that—

Pausing again, Cian tried to decide how to finish that. He scrubbed a hand through his short hair. While lowering his hand back to his keyboard, he tipped his head to the side and cracked his neck. Cian plowed forward. After all, he could never get what he wanted if he didn't try.

I feel like I know you. I feel a chemistry that goes beyond a computer screen. I want the chance to see if it's like that in person.

Cian hit enter and leaned back in his chair. Resting his hands on the armrests, he tapped the fingers of his right hand on the padding restlessly. He stared at the screen, mentally willing Praerna to agree.

Unfortunately, that wasn't what came across the screen.

Wow. I am so flattered. So very, very flattered. You have no idea. But I really can't. I told you about the strict interaction policy that my leaders have in place. It's there for a reason. I promise. And, no, before you ask, I'm not in prison or anything. It's really for our safety.

Plus, I know I never really said, but I've loved talking online because I don't look like you. I'm . . . disfigured. I look different than you. I was born this way. Going in public is impossible for me. Please understand.

Disappointment crashed through Cian. Rubbing his jaw, he read the words twice. He shifted in his seat and felt a twinge in his thigh. Cian lowered his hand to his leg and gently massaged the bumpy skin through his sweats.

Cian lowered his gaze to his covered limb, thinking about the deeply marred flesh underneath the fabric. While he'd touched lightly on his background—that he'd been medically discharged from the military—he hadn't gone into specifics. Cian thought maybe he should. Perhaps it would help.

Returning his hands to the keys, Cian began typing once more.

I understand disfigurement. I understand scars. I mentioned being in the military. Remember?

Surprise filled Cian as he read Praerna's quick response.

I remember. Being in the military is a detriment, to be honest.

Seriously? Cian quickly typed the word, his curiosity piquing. *Why?*

Damn. Most people are pretty respectful and grateful to ex-military. We put our lives on the line so people can enjoy a life of freedom. Why would it be a detriment?

Praerna's answer appeared on his screen in segments, as if he was worried about what he'd just shared.

Sorry.

Didn't mean to offend.

It's just . . . sometimes . . .

Um, groups like us . . . that are different . . . can be persecuted by those who don't understand tolerance for those different.

Sometimes, the military has been used to hurt us.

Cian frowned at the screen. He couldn't imagine why anyone would want to hurt a reclusive group. Unless —

Are you all doing something illegal?

He'd heard of groups doing illegal things in the name of religion. He sure hoped that wasn't what was going on in whatever community Praerna lived in.

No!

Praerna's response came quick.

Absolutely not.

We always follow the rules of the country we live in. Easier to stay left alone that way.

"Ooookay." Cian thought that was an odd thing to say. "Damn. It really does sound like he's part of some kind of reclusive religious community."

Cian wasn't certain how he felt about that. On the one hand, he felt everyone had the right to choose to worship any deity they chose, as long as they didn't use their faith to hurt others. On the other hand, Cian had seen truly horrible things done to others in the name of religion.

Except, Cian realized Praerna's people didn't seem like that sort. From the sounds of it, they just wanted to be left alone to practice ... whatever they practiced. Cian was inclined to believe his friend that they weren't breaking any laws, so he didn't know why they worried they would get into trouble.

Unable to help himself, Cian typed, *Can I ask you a personal question?*

Um. Sure. But I reserve the right not to answer.

Of course. That's always your right. Cian had to smile. *Not like I can force you.*

Then shoot.

Cian couldn't help but smile even as he typed his next question.

Does your community frown on homosexual relationships? Is that why you don't want to meet me?

Another thought hit Cian, and he realized it was also viable. He grinned as a low chuckle escaped.

Or are you actually a woman?

Because if that's the case, I should tell you that I'm bisexual.

Cian added a couple of winky smileys after that comment.

Seeing several roll-on-the-floor-laughing smileys with tears coming out of its eyes appear on his screen, Cian arched one brow. *Huh. What does that mean?* Cian found out quickly enough.

No. I'm a male, and my clutch totally doesn't care about that sort of thing. We're led by a pair of men. They're totally in love with each other. It's truly lovely to see. Gives me hope for the future.

Cian felt a wealth of amusement, enjoying Praerna's playfulness. A second later, a surge of jealousy caused his gut to churn. He sucked in a sharp breath upon feeling the intensity of it. Cian wanted Praerna to have that hope for the future with him. His comment obviously meant he was open to the idea of a relationship.

Then we should meet, Praerna.

Cian couldn't help but press the issue. He couldn't remember the last time he'd felt jealousy, and he wanted the chance to prove himself to the friendly personality he'd become infatuated with.

I know you're worried about what you look like, but please, don't be.

Glancing at his leg again, Cian winced. He typed swiftly, trying to reassure the man.

I only reminded you about my being in the military because I have plenty of scars of my own. My convoy was hit by bad guys, and IED fragments tore through my right side. My thigh was pretty churned up. It's healed now. As much as it can be, anyway. But it's not pretty. And I sure have my fair share of scars. Please, give us a chance to see if we're as compatible in person as we are online.

Cian forced his fingers to still. Staring at the screen, he waited . . . and waited.

sigh

I wish it were that simple . . . but it's not.

Please don't think that you having scars would cause an issue for me. It wouldn't. I just . . . I can't. I'm sorry.

Before Cian could come up with another argument, more words appeared.

I'm gonna go now. I'll, uh . . . I'll talk to you later.

"No," Cian muttered.

A second later, however, the green icon indicating Praerna was online switched to red.

"Shit." Cian slouched in his seat. Resting his head against the seat cushion, he stared at the ceiling. "Why'd you have to push, asshole?"

With a shake of his head, Cian let out a deep sigh. He knew the answer to that. He liked getting his way, and he was damn infatuated with the person he spoke with on a daily basis.

"I'll apologize tomorrow," Cian vowed to himself. "We'll get back to just chatting for a few weeks before I try again."

With that promise in mind, Cian began powering down his gear.

Except, the next day, Praerna didn't show up at their usual time . . . or at all that evening. Cian fell asleep in his computer chair, waking the next morning with a crick in his neck.

For the next three days, Cian watched for Praerna, disappointment and sadness making his chest ache more and more with each day that passed and he didn't see his online friend.

On the fourth day, those emotions switched to anger and frustration. The man could have at least said goodbye. He could have told him not to broach the subject again and continue to communicate with him.

Praerna hadn't even logged into the game they'd been playing together.

For the next week, Cian did his best to push Praerna out of his mind. He did his work-out regimen faithfully, keeping what little muscle was left in his right thigh in shape. While Cian would always walk with a limp and — if leaving home — a cane, at least he'd retained the ability to walk. So many of his fellow servicemen weren't so lucky.

Cian met a fellow retired army ranger — Tyler Dravrin — at a nearby gun range. They fired off several hundred rounds, making bets, shooting the shit, and joshing each other. After that, they went for pizza and beers.

With a bucket of hot wings on the table between them and a pizza on the way, Cian relaxed in his seat and took a sip of his beer. He lowered it to the table. Seeing Tyler's intense scrutiny, Cian arched one brow in silent question.

"You're brooding about something," Tyler stated, narrowing his eyes a little as he tipped his head to the side a smidge. "What is it?"

Cian recognized the look. His fellow serviceman intended to pick at him until he shared. Tyler always loved a puzzle, and he'd been able to read not only Cian but the others in their unit. Tyler had a gift when it came to people.

Heaving a sigh, Cian grabbed one of the two small plates

and a fork. "You know how I enjoy online games?" He began forking several hot wings onto his plate, glancing intermittently at Tyler in the process.

As Tyler followed suit, choosing his own wings, he nodded. "Yep. Heard you say it was a good stress relief to get away from the shit of the world."

"Right." Cian grabbed one of the two tubs of blue cheese dressing. "Well, a few months ago, I met someone on one of the games. We started talking. A lot." After dunking a drumette into the blue cheese, Cian paused and focused on Tyler. "Every day. I really like him. I asked to meet him."

Tyler froze midchew of the bite of chicken he'd just taken, so Cian tore into his own wing and waited. It didn't take long.

A second later, Tyler swallowed his mouthful. "Huh." He waved at Cian with a couple of fingers. "From your look, it didn't go well. Was he not who he'd presented himself to be?"

Shaking his head, Cian admitted, "It never got that far. He said no and stopped talking to me."

"Tough break." Tyler took another bite of food, staring at him as he chewed.

Cian nodded, furrowing his brows as he focused on his own food.

"You're damn disappointed," Tyler commented, picking up his beer. Before taking a swig, he asked, "You want me to help you find him?"

Snapping his attention back to Tyler, Cian fought against the heat that threatened to rise up his neck. "I already tried," he admitted gruffly. "His IP is encrypted."

Anytime Cian wasn't focused on something, his thoughts had turned to Praerna. He'd mentally rewound every conversation they'd had. His heart would flutter in his chest, and sadness would sink into his bones.

Cian had given in to temptation and attempted to track Praerna's handle. He hadn't gotten very far. While he wasn't a bad hacker, his online friend had been better, shielding himself and his location.

Tyler scoffed, a smirk curving his lips. "You know I'm way better than you," he teased. Leaning forward, narrowing his brown eyes as he smirked, Tyler told him, "It's been a while since I've had a chance to test my skills. Let me help you find him."

Hesitating, Cian took a drink of beer, washing down his bite of food. His desire warred with his respect for Praerna's privacy. He wanted to meet the man so damn bad . . . but what if it blew up in his face?

Maybe Praerna is actually married.

But why wouldn't he have just told me?

Wait. Praerna made that comment about hope for the future in regards to his boss being in a relationship with another man.

He's still looking for his special someone.

I want that man to be me.

Meeting Tyler's patient expression, Cian nodded. "Okay."

Tyler chuckled while grinning. "Sweet." He leaned back in his seat, his gaze straying to something over Cian's left shoulder. "After pizza, we'll head to my place."

The waiter arrived and placed their pie on the table. After confirming around round of beers, he headed off again.

Cian and Tyler dug into the pizza.

Anticipation flooded Cian with each bite. As delicious as the pizza was, he couldn't wait to get out of there.

CHAPTER TWO

Praerna knelt beside the flower bed. Using a small garden rake, he tilled the dirt. Once he'd finished preparing the bed, he set the rake aside and slid the flat of chrysanthemums closer toward him.

For a few seconds, Praerna admired the different varieties of flowers—some were a reddish-brown color, others yellowish, and others were white. Each had long and thin petals, tube-like, that went off in all directions. The pretty, elegant-looking chrysanthemums fell into the category of spider blooms due to the way their petals were long and slender, almost spider-leg like.

While Praerna wasn't a big fan of spiders—he'd had to clean way too many cobwebs while under his clutch's prior chieftain—he still admired the lovely flowers.

I wonder if Cyber likes flowers.

Praerna growled softly under his breath.

Damn it. I should not be thinking about CyberHuntsman.

It'd been nearly three weeks since Praerna had broken communication with the human. While it had hurt, he knew it had been necessary. Praerna had loved talking with Cyber every morning—his own morning anyway. It had made him feel sort of normal—somehow part of the world.

As a gargoyle, Praerna couldn't go out in the open. His kind was the one species of paranormal that didn't have a human form until after they'd met and bonded with their mate—the one person who was the other half of their soul. Praerna longed to meet that person.

When Praerna's clutch had been under the cruel, tyrannical rule of Chieftain Grecian, no one had found their mate. He'd given up hope of ever finding that special someone. Praerna had known something would need to change in order for him to get his chance.

To that end, Praerna had secretly worked with other small gargoyles, coordinating acts of defiance against the larger class of gargoyles. Chieftain Grecian had believed that the big gargoyles—the ones with large statures and wings coming out of their backs—should rule the smaller ones—what they called the wingless ones. Praerna was one of those—shorter, standing five-foot-eight, with a slender frame. Instead of real wings, they had wingskins and bone-spurs. The bone-spurs were three cartilage-type appendages which normally rested hidden along their ribs. When their bone-spurs extended from their sides, they would stretch the extra, billowy flaps of skin that ran along their sides. That allowed them to catch the wind and updrafts and fly.

Fortunately, not all of the large gargoyles had agreed with Chieftain Grecian's ideology. An enforcer named Kinsey had had a small gargoyle as a brother—Conchlin. With the help of their mother, Wendy, Conchlin had escaped their clutch, moving to one in another state. He'd found his mate there.

From what Praerna had heard, Kinsey had thought he, his father, his middle brother, and Chieftain Grecian were going to congratulate him. That hadn't happened. Chieftain Grecian and the others had tried to steal Conchlin's mate using an old law. It hadn't worked, but Kinsey had been disgusted.

Through a little good fortune and Fate's blessing, Kinsey had managed to beat Chieftain Grecian in a fair fight—presided over by a gargoyle elder.

Snapping his attention back to his task at hand, Praerna shook his head. He had a dozen flowers to plant in this bed alone before moving on to the next. Praerna had a total of eight beds that he was supposed to finish that evening. Then the rest of the night would be his own.

Except, I'm not certain what I'll do with it.

For the past year, Praerna had filled his spare time with online gaming. He loved the interaction and getting to chat with others. Around six months before, Praerna had started conversing with *CyberHuntsman.*

Too bad he's human. I would have loved to actually meet him.

Pushing thoughts of the human who'd become a great friend from his mind, Praerna planted the garden bed. They were installing a large garden maze similar to the one where Conchlin resided. Under Grecian's rule, the exterior grounds had been neglected, falling into ruin.

Not anymore, though.

That was Praerna's favorite change. He was no longer required to always stay indoors, cooking, cleaning, and taking care of every menial task the big gargoyles considered beneath them. Instead, Praerna enjoyed hours outside as a groundskeeper.

Praerna loved gardening, even when it involved removing excessive amounts of overgrowth. He'd helped clear all the weeds and trim the overgrown bushes around the estate house. Praerna had looked up online how to hedge bushes, and he'd even learned topiary.

So very cool.

Cyber had loved hearing me talk about the different animals I'd cut into the bushes.

With a sigh, Praerna returned his attention to planting. Working with the soil eased his heart a little. He never could have anticipated how much he would miss his daily chats with Cyber.

The man had wanted to meet Praerna, and he knew that could never happen. While Praerna had ignored the fact that Cyber had been in the military, he hadn't really forgotten. If someone from the military learned of their gargoyle clutch—

even someone ex-military—he or she could still cause problems. Praerna had heard all those sayings about once a marine always a marine. He didn't know if Cyber had been a marine or not, but he figured that sort of motto carried over into other divisions—meaning, Cyber would have access to people who could really cause problems for them if he reacted poorly to the knowledge of the paranormal.

Moot point, anyway. That's why I cut ties. So he'll never know.

Praerna heard his phone chime, telling him he had a text. Grabbing a damp cloth he always kept handy while working with dirt, he wiped his fingers and claws. He set the cloth aside and picked up his phone.

Staring at the text, Praerna furrowed his eyebrow ridges. It was from Second Destrawn.

Contact me at your earliest convenience.

Knowing there was no reason to delay calling their clutch's second in command—plus, he knew that his imagination would come up with all sorts of weird scenarios—Praerna called the male.

"Hello, Praerna," Destrawn greeted, his voice deep and a little rough. "Thank you for getting back to me so quickly. I know you're outside working this evening."

The large, dark-green second was a new edition to their clutch. After Kinsey had taken over, the new chieftain had needed a number of strong gargoyles to create a brand-new inner circle of leadership. Elder Vermidian, who'd presided over the takeover, had assisted with his own guards until a suitable second, as well as a number of enforcers, could be brought in.

Destrawn had proved to be fair, if a little on the brusque side. He took his duties seriously, caring for the clutch while backing Kinsey and offering counsel. To Destrawn's credit, Fate had even blessed him with a vampire mate—Sorbin.

"Yes, Second," Praerna replied dutifully. "I'm planting flower beds, so could easily hear my phone."

"Are you nearly finished with whatever bed you're working on?"

Praerna looked over the bed as well as his supplies. "Well, yes, this one. I have two more to plant here," he admitted. Quickly, he added, "I'm supposed to do seven more after this one."

The night was young, and he'd just started. He hoped the second wouldn't think he was working too slow or had been busy goofing off.

As if reading his mind, Destrawn rumbled, "Understandable. The sun only set an hour and a half ago."

Unbonded gargoyles, such as Praerna, slept during the day as stone statues. Something they referred to as roost. They woke at sunset, and the first hour was their own time, using it to clean up, relax, eat, and prepare for their day.

"When you're done with that bed, we need you to come to Chieftain Kinsey's office," Destrawn told him. "A situation has risen that we hope you can help us sort out."

"O-Okay. Yes, Second."

Praerna did his best to keep the squeak out of his voice, but he wasn't totally successful. In the past, getting called into the chieftain's office was *never* a good thing.

"Relax, Praerna," Destrawn encouraged, his deep voice taking on a soothing quality. "We just need to get some information from you. Not the end of the world."

"O-Okay," he muttered again. "I-I'll be there soon."

"Good." With that, Destrawn hung up.

For several heartbeats, Praerna sat on the ground, frozen. He felt his breath catch in his chest. A trickle of fear tracked down his spine.

Then Praerna forced himself to take a deep breath, then another. He reminded himself that Chieftain Kinsey was nothing like Grecian. Kinsey wouldn't beat him for some trumped-up misdeed.

"No sense in putting off the inevitable," Praerna muttered, quickly getting back to work. "I'm sure it's nothing."

Praerna didn't really believe that, though. Regardless of leadership, getting called to the chieftain was *never* nothing. He could only hope that whatever it was, there was a simple explanation and a simple conversation would clear up the matter.

With that hope clutched tightly in his mind, Praerna swiftly planted the remaining two chrysanthemums. He picked up his planting supplies and hurried to a large garden shed. Praerna moved around the recently purchased small tractor with a lawn mowing attachment to the racks on the left wall and hung up his tools.

Jogging across the lawn, Praerna rushed to his room. The estate had undergone extensive remodeling after Kinsey had taken over. He'd combined rooms and added bathrooms. Now, instead of sharing a small, bare-necessities washroom with another small gargoyle, Praerna—and all the others similar to himself—had their own larger suite and a nice bathroom complete with a separate tub and shower.

Chieftain Kinsey had spoken with each of them, allowing them all to share in the design, so it could be made to their specifications—within reason, anyway.

Praerna quickly scrubbed his arms and face, cleaning them of dirt and sweat. Unable to help himself, he took a second to run his fingers through his pale green hair. Once he was satisfied with the spiky style, he hurried from his room.

Leaving that wing of the estate—there were three of them—Praerna entered the one that contained Chieftain Kinsey's quarters and office. The second, the top three enforcers, and the head tracker also resided there. While that had been standard for Chieftain Grecian, too, it had just worked out that way when Kinsey had taken over because those were the rooms that were open when the others had arrived.

As Praerna climbed the stairs to the second floor, an interesting scent caught his attention. He paused and sniffed deeply. The aroma reminded him of a mixture of fresh pine with a hint of gun oil.

Praerna didn't know why, but he found it delicious. His stomach fluttered, and to his shock, his groin even warmed. He had the oddest desire to make his chieftain wait so he could track down the source.

Shaking his head, Praerna resumed climbing the stairs. Nothing good ever came of making a chieftain wait, even one as understanding as Kinsey seemed to be. He reached the second floor where the offices were and started that way.

The door to Second Destrawn's office opened, and the large green gargoyle stepped out. The male offered the slightest of smiles with a chin bob of acknowledgment before beckoning with a couple of black-clawed fingers. He turned and went to the next door.

The inner circle's lounge.

Praerna hadn't been in there since he'd discussed with the chieftain his preferences for his suite's renovations. Some of his nerves eased. The space was used for informal meetings, budget strategy, and relaxing by the inner circle and their mates—those who had them, anyway.

Destrawn opened the door and stepped back, silently urging him to enter.

Stepping into the room, Praerna didn't know if he felt relief or more tension. Not only was Chieftain Kinsey in the room, but he also had his mate, Jimmy, curled up next to him on a small sofa. His pregnant mate was pressed against him, his baby bump just beginning to show, so he could no longer go out in public.

Along with them was Head Enforcer Sethnos. The unbonded gargoyle rested on another small sofa. His powder-gray hide almost gleamed in the lamp-light, and he had his black wings draped over the back of the piece of furniture.

Lathe sat on a sofa off to the side, a laptop balanced on his thighs. The green-eyed vampire had joined them from a nearby coven that many of the clutch's gargoyles had mated into. Although, Lathe's gargoyle mate—Holden—had come from the clutch where Kinsey's brother, Conchlin, currently resided. Holden sat next to Lathe, his deep purple arm draped over the back as he leaned close to the vampire.

"Come in, Praerna," Chieftain Kinsey urged, smiling at him. He indicated an open chair to his left. "Have a seat. We have a couple of questions for you."

"Of course, Chieftain." Praerna quickly obeyed, pleased that he'd managed to get his voice to come out even. After sitting, he folded his hands on his lap and glanced around. "Anything I can do to help."

"Thank you, Praerna." Kinsey smiled encouragingly. With his arm around Jimmy's body, he rubbed that hand over his mate's belly in a way that looked absent, yet protective. "This morning, we received reports about a human that checked into a bed and breakfast in the nearby town, Lake Point. A man named Cian." Arching one white eyebrow ridge, Kinsey asked, "Does that name ring a bell?"

Praerna shook his head slowly. "No, sir," he replied. "I don't know anyone named Cian."

"Well, he knows you." Lathe looked up from his laptop and spun it around, showing a picture of a man. "Recognize him now?"

Leaning forward, Praerna took in Cian's features. His heartrate picked up, and his breath caught. He felt his pulse begin to race.

The man was . . . *gorgeous*. He had pale-brown skin, brown eyes, and high cheek bones. His dark-brown hair had been cut short—military short—giving a smidge of harshness to his features. The man wasn't smiling in the picture, but Praerna still found his attention snagged by his full lips.

"No," Praerna whispered. "I don't know him." Unable to help himself, he murmured, "But I'd sure like to."

"Well, you're going to get your wish," Kinsey declared. "Because Cian Huntsman is here, demanding to see you."

Jolting, Praerna straightened in his seat. Gaping, he shook his head once as shock flooded him. His blood drained from his face, and his heart began to pound for a new reason.

"*Huntsman?*" Praerna barely managed to get the word past his lips.

Sethnos nodded once. "His name is Cian Huntsman." He crossed his arms over his broad chest. "Now do you know the human?"

Praerna nodded, too shocked to get words past his throat. *CyberHuntsman is here.*

How is that possible?

CHAPTER THREE

Cian stood near the window, staring at the front lawn. Clutching his cane in his right hand, he rested a little of his weight on it. His thigh ached slightly, tired from riding his *Honda NC750X DCT* motorcycle across three states. Cian knew he should have driven his *Jeep Cherokee*, but the gorgeous weather had suckered him in.

And now, my thigh is paying for it. Although, if on the off chance I can take Praerna for a ride, feeling his arms around me, his chest pressing against my back, it'll be worth any price.

Besides, Cian had found a bed and breakfast in town that offered a jetted tub. The extra cost was well worth the soothing it had been to his muscles the prior evening. He thought about the events of the last day and a half and hoped they wouldn't get him into hot water.

At least Tyler knows where I am and will search for me if I miss my check-in.

Cian had arrived the day before and had spent half that time scouting the area. Picking up a few groceries to stock in his room, he'd dropped a comment about visiting the local commune while checking out. The woman behind the counter had appeared confused and hadn't commented.

Fortunately, the waiter serving him dinner had seemed a bit more knowledgeable. He'd laughed and told him, "I don't think I've ever heard them called a commune before. I thought the guys in the mansion were a nudist colony or something." With a smirk, the waiter added, "After all, no one ever gets to go near the back of the property without invitation."

A nudist colony?

Cian had barely resisted laughing at the waiter. Instead, he'd confirmed the direction.

After driving so many miles—from his home in the foothills of eastern Missouri—Cian had enjoyed sleeping in until nearly noon. He'd taken his time getting up, going through his full exercise regime, before taking a short soak in the tub. Eating the food he'd purchased the prior day, he hadn't even needed to leave the room.

Finally, when the sun had begun to sink in the sky, Cian had sought out the location of the commune. He'd had to drive down one side road after another, turning around many times. Tyler hadn't been able to give him an exact address, just a general location.

Cian had watched the sun sink in the sky as the ache in his leg grew. He'd been worried that he would have to return to town and resume his search the next day when he'd spotted a security camera in a tree. Pressing on, Cian had seen a second, then a third, confirming that he was probably in the right location.

The massive mansion-like structure that had appeared between the trees had been a surprise. Cian parked beneath the portico and swung from his bike. His right thigh had nearly buckled, and he'd had to hurry and pull his cane from the holder he'd designed for it. Cian had just finished confirming his firearm was safely hidden beneath his leather jacket in a shoulder holster when the front door had opened, revealing a massive man with long, black hair.

"Are you lost?" the guy had asked bluntly. "Need directions?"

"No, I'm not lost," Cian replied, removing his helmet from his head one-handed. He rested it on the handlebar. Eyeing the bruiser of a man—*he has to be some sort of security*—Cian watched for signs of recognition as he asked, "I'm looking for Praerna. Is he available?"

The man's dark gray eyes narrowed just a smidge. "I can't imagine Praerna is expecting you," he rumbled as he swept his gaze up and down Cian. "Why do you want him?"

"Good. So he does live here." Cian smiled grimly at the huge male. "I'd like to see him."

"Why?" The man crossed his arms over his chest as he leaned a massive shoulder against the frame of the open doorway. He looked to be settling in, as if he had all day to wait for Cian to answer. "Who are you?"

Recalling the adage about catching more flies with honey, Cian began limping toward the man. He stopped a few paces away and switched his cane to his left hand. Then he held out his right one.

"I'm Cian Huntsman," Cian told him. "I lost contact with Praerna a few weeks ago, and I'm worried about him. I just want to see him . . . for my own peace of mind."

"You're claiming Praerna knows you, Cian?" The man slowly reached out and took Cian's hand. For such a large male, he offered a good handshake, not trying to dominate with his strength, before releasing him. "How long have you known each other?"

"We've been friends for about six months."

Cian decided that was true enough. He considered Praerna his friend, and he wanted more from the man, if at all possible. Cian returned his cane to his right hand and leaned on it, flexing his right thigh lightly, his need to rest it growing quickly now that he was on his feet.

The man's attention flicked to Cian's leg, his cane, and finally to his jacket. He'd obviously caught Cian's discomfort.

Instead of commenting on it, however, he stated, "I'm Destrawn. You can come in and wait, but we don't allow anyone to meet our members unless we've run a background check on them." Destrawn's gaze flitted toward the growing darkness beyond him. "It could be at least an hour before my boss comes to a decision, and you'll have to meet with him first."

"Fair enough," Cian replied, taking a step forward.

Destrawn held up one medium-brown hand. "And you'll have to leave the firearm in your motorcycle."

Cian hesitated. He hadn't even been aware that Destrawn had noticed it. Glancing over the large man's broad-shouldered frame covered in a polo shirt and jeans, Cian wondered if the security guy was carrying.

Just how safe will I be?

His thick lips quirking into a wry smile, Destrawn told him, "I guarantee you'll be leaving here safely, Cian."

Realizing he had to take Destrawn at his word, Cian nodded once. "Okay." Then he'd limped back to his motorcycle and locked his pistol into a side saddlebag.

Two hours later, Cian felt his bladder twinge. He'd enjoyed two cups of excellent coffee doctored with a little flavored creamer. The brand was one he didn't recognize, and he'd taken a picture of it with his phone so he could look it up online.

Cian had been left waiting in a nicely appointed salon with comfortable sofas and chairs. There was even a fire in the fireplace. Not only had coffee and other drinks been provided, but there had been several trays of pastries, meats, and cheeses.

Everything appeared to be high-end, and the food he'd enjoyed had been delicious.

And now, I'd really like to go to the men's room.

Cian wondered if he would get into trouble for leaving the room. After he'd met with a man named Kinsey—no last name offered—a slender man with dark hair came in with the trolley of food and drink. Cian hadn't seen anyone after that, and it'd been nearly two hours.

Limping toward the door, Cian placed the empty coffee mug on a side table as he passed it. He stood before the door for a second, hesitating. Cian heaved a sigh while rolling his eyes and grimacing.

As Cian reached for the doorknob, he saw it turn. He had just enough time to move back a step before the door swung open. A lean man with sandy-blond hair arched one brow as he saw him.

"Uh," Cian began, feeling a little embarrassed. Quickly, he explained, "I was going to try to flag someone down. Can you show me to a men's room?"

Chuckling softly, the man smirked at him. "Of course." He took a step backward, beckoning with one finger. "This way." As Cian followed him, the man peered over his shoulder at him, saying, "I'm Sorbin, by the way. Destrawn's partner."

Damn. The big bruiser is gay?

Cian wouldn't have guessed that.

And I should know better than to judge a book by its cover.

"Nice to meet you," Cian responded, for lack of a better response.

"I'd say the same to you, but I suppose that remains to be seen." Sorbin paused before an unmarked door. "This door leads to a recreation room. It's empty right now. There's a bathroom in there. First door to the right," he told him. "Return to the salon as soon as you're done." As if Cian needed extra incentive, Sorbin added, "I believe Praerna will be there waiting for you when you get back."

Cian quickly nodded, even though he would have returned without the order. "Thank you." With his bladder urging him forward, he headed inside.

As Cian limped swiftly across the room, he couldn't help but take in the nice space. There were a number of comfortable-looking couches clustered around a huge TV, which hung on the far wall. A bar spanned part of another wall, and judging by the bottles on the shelves behind it, it was well stocked. There was a pool table and a foosball table, as well as an air hockey table. A few video games plus a dart board was along another wall.

Shaking his head, Cian wondered who these people were and where they got their money. Everything he'd seen appeared of good quality and high-end. He had no idea what he was stumbling into.

Cian quickly used the john, relieving his bladder. After washing and drying his hands, he grabbed his cane and headed back the way he'd come. He could hear the soft rumble of voices coming from the salon he'd been waiting in.

"Are you certain, Praerna?" a male voice asked that Cian was almost sure was Kinsey.

"Yes."

The soft melodic voice that answered caused heat to stir in Cian's blood.

What would that man's voice whispering in my ear sound like?

"He's my mate," the man, Praerna, spoke again. "I had no idea!"

"You wouldn't until you scented him," Kinsey replied, sounding understanding. "We'll help you get this sorted. The fact that he came all this way tells us that Fate is already hard at work."

Cian paused outside the door, uncertainty filling him.

Mate? Fate? What the hell are they talking about?

"No sense loitering out here, Cian."

Cian pivoted, stumbling as his thigh twinged. Resting his left hand on the wall, he peered up at Destrawn, taking in his smirking countenance. The big man glanced at his thigh and the cane again as his expression softened.

"You need something for the pain?" the big man offered. "I can call the doc."

"No," Cian grumbled, annoyed at his weakness. "It's just

24

tired."

Lifting his hands in placation, Destrawn offered, "Let us know if that changes. I know he has some nice electronic massaging pads. I used them before meeting my mate." With a waggle of his eyebrows, he added, "I got lucky. Sorbin knows massage. Great foreplay."

Cian opened his mouth, then closed it again, having no idea how to respond to that.

Ooookay. That's more than I need to know about a complete stranger.

Destrawn chuckled, the sound deep and low. "Shocked you." The man patted his shoulder lightly. "Well, you'll get used to our openness about such things." Then Destrawn waved toward the doorway again. "In you go. It's time you learned how deep the rabbit hole goes."

Confused and concerned, Cian remained frozen for a few seconds. He watched as Destrawn rocked back on one foot, appearing far more relaxed than when he'd first met him a couple of hours before. Cian wondered at the change.

Must have been the background check.

Cian realized he didn't really have a choice. Plus, he knew Praerna was in the room, and he really wanted to meet the man. Planting his cane, Cian pushed off the wall and started moving again. Anticipation flooded him, and his heartrate sped up.

Damn. Can't remember the last time I was looking forward to meeting someone so much.

Doing his best to keep his breathing — and his gait — even, Cian entered the room. The trolley was still there, although someone had added liquor bottles and tumblers to it. Someone had also put up a folding partition screen.

Cian could just make out the silhouette of a slender figure behind it.

Is that Praerna?

Kinsey stood in the room as did the man introduced as

Jimmy, his husband. While Cian would never say it, if Jimmy had been a woman, he would have pegged her as pregnant. Jimmy sported what looked like a baby bump.

Hope that's not a cancer tumor and he's just a little fat.

"So you came all the way from Missouri, uninvited, to check up on Praerna, whom you claim is a friend," Kinsey stated, guiding Jimmy toward one of the love seats. "That was a bit of a stretch, but I'd be interested in meeting Tyler. Our computer expert, Lathe, would like to collaborate with him."

"How do you know about Tyler?" Cian asked warily.

Taking a seat next to Jimmy, Kinsey rested his arm along the back, placing his hand proprietarily on his husband's shoulder. "Once Lathe had your name, he did some fancy computer shit that I can't follow." Kinsey shrugged. "Suffice it to say, he discovered Tyler's trace on our IP address and backtracked to the man." Waving the hand holding a tumbler of . . . something, Kinsey shook his head. "That's for later." He pointed at the screen. "Praerna told us that he broke off contact with you because you wanted to meet." Kinsey's deep green eyes twinkled as he smiled. "But that wasn't good enough for you. You decided to come find him. And now that you're here, we know why."

"You do?" The words were out of Cian's mouth before he could think better of them. He frowned at the big man. "I told you the truth. I came to meet Praerna and make certain he's safe."

Scoffing softly, Kinsey nodded. "Indeed." His expression sobered. "Praerna did warn you that the people here are . . . different."

Cian nodded. "Yes. He mentioned that the people here have some abnormalities. Uh . . . disfigurements, I think is the word he used."

"Damn it, Praerna," Destrawn grumbled from where he stood leaning against the wall near the door. "Did you seriously call yourself disfigured?"

"I-I wasn't c-certain how else to explain." Praerna's soft tenor filled the air, causing Cian's body to flush with the heat of arousal. When Praerna continued, Cian's gut clenched with the pleasure of the sound of his voice. "Cyber wanted to meet me, and I didn't know how else to dissuade him." Praerna's voice grew even quieter as he whispered, "I just wanted to keep talking to him."

"It's fine, Praerna," Kinsey stated soothingly. He focused on Cian, his expression serious. "You were warned that we are different. And now you'll learn why." Without looking away from Cian, Kinsey ordered, "It's time to come out, Praerna."

"Okay." Praerna sounded tentative as hell.

Cian took a step forward, anticipation rushing through him as he watched the form ease near the edge of the screen.

When Praerna appeared, Cian's body rushed hot for a whole new reason.

Shock.

Before him stood . . . something . . . some creature of some kind. The beast stood about five-foot-eight and had light-purple skin that looked thick, even a little bumpy, like a leathery hide. It had a square-like jaw, and the tips of canines peeked over his lips. The creature's eyes were an odd, vibrant yellow with a vertical pupil, like a reptile. It even had green hair on its head that looked artfully fashioned into a short, spikey style.

The creature lifted a hand in a half-wave, causing Cian to notice the black claws tipping his fingers. "Hi." Praerna's soft voice came from the beast.

"Holy shit." Cian couldn't have stopped the words, even if he'd tried.

When Cian took a step backward, the creature appeared to wince as it hunched its shoulders.

The back of Cian's good leg hit the sofa behind him, and he sat down heavily, even as the urge to flee hit him.

"Cian." Kinsey barked his name, drawing his attention. The big man stared at him solemnly. "This place is the home of a gargoyle clutch." He indicated Praerna. "Praerna is a gargoyle. That's why he declined meeting you."

Disbelief flooded Cian, but he couldn't deny what was right before his very eyes. Swallowing hard, he managed to get a little moisture into his throat. He met Kinsey's gaze and asked, "Why would you tell me?"

After all, with a secret this big, surely they have ways of sending people on their way without telling them.

And I'm not certain I want to know.

CHAPTER FOUR

Praerna watched Cian drop to the sofa, and he barely refrained from running to the human's side. Clenching his clawed hands against his sides, he hugged himself tightly. He knew Cian wouldn't welcome his touch, and that knowledge caused an ache to start in his gut.

Suddenly, the wonderful breakfast of biscuits and gravy he'd eaten a couple of hours before didn't seem like such a good idea. He swallowed hard, forcing down the bile. Feeling Sorbin touch his shoulder, he looked up at the vampire to see him offering him an opened bottle of water.

Taking it gratefully, Praerna took a sip, then a bigger one.

"We're telling you this for a number of reasons, Cian." Kinsey answered Cian's muttered question. "First off, Fate brought you here for a reason."

"Fate?"

Cian glanced at Kinsey for a second before returning his attention back to Praerna. He couldn't seem to tear his gaze away from him for long, and Praerna hoped that was a good thing. Although, the wide dilation of his dark brown eyes, coupled with the heavy scent of unease filling the room, didn't lend him much faith in that.

"You all believe in Fate?" Cian's black brows furrowed as he narrowed his eyes. "Why?"

Kinsey chuckled as he spread the arm not holding Jimmy wide. "You're sitting in the home of a gargoyle clutch, and you wonder why we believe in Fate?" His full lips curved into a smirk. "Surely you realize now that there are many more things on this earth than just humans."

Pursing his lips, Cian blew out a slow breath. "Gargoyles," he whispered, obviously attempting to wrap his mind around that. "Praerna is a gargoyle." Raking his gaze over him, Cian licked his lips. He seemed to be searching for some frame of reference, for he finally asked, "Where did you guys come from? And how did you learn our technology?"

Destrawn snorted. "What? You think we're from another planet or something?" He shook his head as he stared at him. "We've been here all along, Cian. Humans have never been alone on planet Earth."

"We haven't?" Cian was clearly having a hard time wrapping his mind around that.

"We just hide," Praerna stated softly. "After all, humans have persecuted every minority group at one time or another." He shrugged. "Some still do. Skin color." Praerna began ticking off things on his fingers. "Body shape. Religion. Sexual orientation. Hell, at this point, whether you drive a motorcycle or not can make people think differently of you." Praerna had noticed the motorcycle outside, and he couldn't recall Cian ever mentioning that he rode.

By the time Praerna finished, Cian was nodding slowly. "Fair enough." He rubbed his right thigh, drawing attention to the way the jeans were indented differently than on his other leg. "Injuries, illnesses, and deformities, too." Cian frowned at Praerna. "But you're not deformed in any way. Are you?" He waved his left hand up and down, indicating Praerna's frame. "This is the way a gargoyle is made?"

Praerna finally felt a real glimmer of hope. He spotted the curiosity in Cian's brown eyes. Plus, he was starting to ask questions.

From what Praerna had heard, asking questions was a step toward acceptance.

As Praerna nodded, murmuring, "Yeah," Kinsey took it a

step further.

"Gargoyles come in two general types."

Then Chieftain Kinsey explained the difference between larger and smaller gargoyles. How some had true wings coming from their shoulder blades. Others had wingskins and bone-spurs. All of them could fly. Kinsey even went on to explain roosting—sleeping during the day as a stone statue.

"Wow, okay. That explains your gaming hours." Cian's lips flitted into a tiny smile even as he nodded. "And I can see how gargoyles would want to keep that a secret. Talk about a vulnerability." He glanced between everyone before focusing on Kinsey. "So . . . you and these others are their security? Like, you protect them during the day?"

"I do." Sorbin raised his hand, winking at him. "But part of that is because Destrawn is my beloved."

"Beloved," Cian repeated, glancing toward Destrawn. "Does that mean husband here?"

Sorbin waggled his hand back and forth. "Nah, not really." He cleared his throat before asking, "Uh, should I drop that bombshell on him, Chieftain? Or don't you think he's ready?"

Cian frowned, perhaps annoyed at being talked about while he was sitting right in front of them.

Kinsey sighed deeply. "We'll need to explain it all eventually. Beloveds, mates, bonding, molting." Smiling encouragingly at Praerna, he asked him, "You were the one in contact with Cian for six months. How much of an information dump do you think he can mentally handle?"

Praerna opened his mouth, then snapped it closed again. He certainly hadn't been ready for his chieftain to ask his opinion on the matter. He couldn't recall any higher-ranking gargoyle doing that to any of them before on matters of such importance.

"Um, well." Praerna met Cian's gaze, offering a tentative smile. "We need to explain a few more things for you to truly understand, Cian." Taking a chance, Praerna eased closer to him. When he saw his human stiffen, he did his best not to feel offended. "I would never hurt you," Praerna murmured softly. "None of us here would."

Praerna paused a few feet away from Cian and told him, "We still need to share why you felt so compelled to make the trip here."

"I was worried about you," Cian immediately claimed. "You cut contact."

"Just worried?" Kinsey countered. "Maybe upset? Sad? Frustrated?"

A muscle ticked in Cian's jaw. "So?"

Taking that as affirmative, Praerna eased onto the sofa next to Cian, keeping a foot of space between them. "Thank you." He smiled at Cian, doing his best to ignore the way his mate held the head of his cane in a white-knuckled grip. "Thank you for worrying about me. For coming here." Praerna read the tension lines in Cian's body and desperately wished he had the courage to hold him, to trill for him, but he feared his human jumping away from him. Instead, he murmured, "I feel so very blessed to have you turn up on our doorstep. I know you don't understand yet, but meeting you . . . is life-changing for me."

"Why is meeting me life-changing, Praerna?" Cian asked softly. His nostrils flared a little as he took in a sharp breath. "And why do I really want to reach out and touch your hide? To see what it feels like?" His gaze sweeping over Praerna's torso, Cian whispered, "And touch your wingskins." His fingers twitched. "To see how soft they are?"

"You're my mate," Praerna blurted, unable to keep in such amazing news. "The other half of my soul. The one person I can bond with, to build a life with. I want to spend the rest of my years figuring out every way to make you happy."

"Mate." Cian whispered the word. Cocking his head, he

glanced around again. "You all have used that term a couple of times." He frowned at Destrawn. "You referred to Sorbin as your mate, and he called you his beloved. To you, it means . . . partner?"

Destrawn nodded once. "A gargoyle uses the word mate to refer to their special someone, the other half of their soul. The person gifted to them by the Fates, so they can bond, build a life together, and not be alone for our very long lifespan." His words were blunt and straightforward. Then he pointed at Cian. "You see, Praerna couldn't come to you. So Fate brought you to him. You, Cian, you are Praerna's mate."

Praerna could see Cian's eyes widening the more Destrawn spoke. His brows rose up his forehead. Even his lips parted, the scent of his disbelief once again intensifying.

Cian snapped his attention to Praerna and stared at him for a few seconds. He opened his mouth, then snapped it shut again. His eyes narrowed, and his expression took on one of disbelief.

"No," Cian mumbled, shaking his head. While Praerna winced, trying not to take offense, since he knew it was a human's knee-jerk reaction to that sort of news, Cian looked around at everyone again. "That can't be right. I'm human."

Jimmy lifted his hand. "Yup. So am I." He pointed his thumb at Kinsey. "Kinsey is the gargoyle in our relationship." Then he pointed at Destrawn. "Just like Destrawn is the gargoyle in his and Sorbin's relationship."

Cian looked at Sorbin. "And you're the human?" He frowned. "How does that even work?" Snapping his attention back to Kinsey, he pointed at Praerna while asking, "And if you're a gargoyle, why don't you look like him? Or like one of the bigger ones you talked about?"

"Don't get up, Chieftain," Destrawn stated with a wave of his hand. He pushed off the wall and grabbed the hem of his polo shirt. "I'll show him."

"And no, actually," Sorbin stated, moving toward the drink trolley. "I'm not a human." With a wink, he picked up a decanter of amber liquid. "Although I can easily pass for one."

"What are you?" Cian asked, glancing from him to Destrawn, who'd draped his shirt over the back of a chair. Destrawn was in the process of unbuttoning his fly, and Cian frowned at Sorbin. "And why is your partner undressing?"

"Gargoyles do not have a human form until *after* they've found and bonded with their mate," Sorbin explained. Continuing, he told him, "Destrawn's about to show you how a mated and bonded gargoyle can change his form. After they go through molt, that is." Holding up his hand, Sorbin quickly added, "Don't worry. We'll explain everything." Then, as if an afterthought, Sorbin added, "And I'm a vampire."

"A vampire." Cian shook his head in clear disbelief. "Of course you are."

"I warned you that you were going to see how far the rabbit hole goes, Alice," Destrawn teased. Smirking, he added, "Now, I'm going to change into my true form." He pointed at Sorbin. "Sorbin has whiskey ready for you in case you need it."

Before Cian could respond, Destrawn returned to his natural gargoyle form. His medium-brown skin darkened to a dark-green shade, becoming a swarthy hide. His shoulders broadened as his frame grew, adding a couple of inches to his height. Tipping his head back, which now sported canines poking over his lips, Destrawn grunted. A second later, his large black wings appeared behind him. Destrawn spread them, as if shaking them out, showcasing their impressive, twelve-foot wingspan.

"Holy shit," Cian whispered. His cane clattered to the floor, and he began to slump.

Praerna grabbed Cian before he could tumble to the floor.

Wrapping his arms around him, he held him close. He trilled softly as he glanced between the others.

"What do I do?" Praerna squeaked, rubbing his palm up and down his mate's cloth-covered chest.

"You're doing it," Jimmy told him, smiling kindly. "Just keep trilling, and when Cian rouses, we'll start explaining again and answer every question he has."

Nodding, Praerna could only do as he'd been told, praying to any god that cared to listen that his mate would wake up receptive to everything they still needed to share.

CHAPTER FIVE

Sitting on the bed in his room at the bed and breakfast, Cian rested his forearms on his thighs. He stared at the TV, but he couldn't have said what was on. Cian had turned it on for background noise.

Instead, Cian's mind whirled with all the information he'd learned that evening. He never would have imagined that paranormals were real. Cian just didn't have that kind of imagination.

Praerna is a gargoyle.

Cian bowed his head and closed his eyes, focusing on his breathing. Recalling the feel of the pale purple male's arms around him, he felt his body react. It had felt shockingly good, and arousal began simmering through his veins just at the memory.

But he's a gargoyle.

Straightening, Cian rubbed his thighs. He stopped with his left hand but continued with his right. His thigh ached lightly with fatigue. Cian knew he should sleep, but he couldn't get his brain to settle.

Cian was actually a little surprised that Kinsey had allowed him to leave. Of course, they all seemed to have a hell of a lot of faith in the fated mate thing they'd told him about. They expected him to uproot his life and mate with Praerna.

Wasn't that what I was prepared to do when I decided to first come out here? If me and Praerna had had the slightest chemistry, I would've done my best to woo him.

But he's a gargoyle.

Cian just couldn't seem to get past that. Rubbing his left hand over his scalp, he groaned softly. Then he flopped backward on the bed and stared at the ceiling.

God, does that make me a racist prick? Just because he's a different species, suddenly I'm not interested?

Except, Cian didn't know how to reconcile everything in his mind. He'd told them he needed time to process. They'd agreed to let him return to the bed and breakfast.

I wonder if they have someone watching me. I promised to keep silent about them. I'm pretty sure they wouldn't have let me leave otherwise.

Cian didn't know how long he lay there before fatigue finally caused him to drift off. When he woke, the faint rays of morning shined through the window. His first thought was of Praerna.

He'll be a stone statue right now. I wonder what that looks like.

Wait? Really? Do I really want to see that?

Cian didn't make it a habit of lying to himself. He had to admit that he did. If he showed up at the estate, would Kinsey allow him to see Praerna's sleeping form?

But if I do that, will they think I'm accepting . . . everything? The whole mate thing? And now I'm back to that.

Groaning softly, Cian pushed to a sitting position. He grimaced as he peered down at himself. Sleeping in regular clothes reminded him too much of his time in the military.

Tugging his shirt over his head, Cian placed it on the mattress. He grimaced just at the thought of removing his jeans and going through his morning exercise regime. Unfortunately, he knew that the consequences would be far worse if he skipped it.

Cian heaved a deep sigh, then unbuttoned and unzipped his fly. Planting his weight on his left leg, he levered his hips up. He quickly shoved his jeans down before plopping his ass back onto the comforter.

Once Cian kicked off his jeans, leaving him in nothing but

his boxer-briefs, he rummaged through his duffel bag, which was still sitting on the left side of the bed. He found his bungee cord with handles attached to each end. Sliding to the floor, Cian got into position and started his morning exercises.

Thirty minutes later, dripping with sweat, Cian panted as he stared at the ceiling. He focused on his breathing, slowly getting it under control. His muscles were warm but not sore, and he relaxed for a couple of moments.

Cian eased to a sitting position, then rolled to his knees. Standing, he felt a measure of relief when his thigh didn't twinge. He tossed the bungee onto the bed beside his duffel bag before rummaging through it to find his bathroom kit.

Then Cian moved slowly toward the bathroom, limping mildly. He placed his kit on the counter and opened it. Pulling out his toothbrush and paste, he started with that before shaving and getting into the shower.

Once clean, Cian returned to the bedroom, a towel wrapped around his waist. He pulled out a fresh set of clothes. After dropping the towel to the floor, he sat on the side of the bed.

As Cian pulled on his underwear, his attention snagged on his right side and thigh. His skin was littered with scars, pale-white spiderwebs of puckered flesh attesting to how much debris had sliced through him. The surface of his thigh rippled and dipped, the muscle underneath having been decimated by shrapnel, leaving only part of it behind. His thighs would always be two different sizes, and his right one wasn't pretty.

But Praerna wants to accept me, no questions asked. He didn't comment about my limp or the cane.

With a deep sigh, Cian shook his head.

I really need to get out of here. I need time away to think. I got the information on why Praerna didn't want to meet me, and now I need to move on.

With that thought in mind, Cian finished dressing. Then he packed up his stuff. He'd paid for the room for another night, but he wasn't worried about trying to get the money back. Instead, Cian would just leave. If anyone was monitoring his movements, they would assume he would be returning that evening.

Probably, anyway.

Cian left his packed bag on his bed and made his way out of his room. Turning left, he scented the breakfast before he saw it. The second story was made up of three suites and a communal area at the back. There was a coffee maker, relaxing seating looking out on a small garden with a water feature, as well as a dining area that could comfortably seat eight. On the bar, his hostess had set up a couple of warming trays as well as one that was chilled.

When Cian had checked in, the hostess asked if he had any dietary restrictions or allergies. He had assured her that he didn't. Cian wasn't a picky eater. Although he did his best to keep his diet clean, avoiding most processed or sugary foods.

To that end, Cian avoided the cinnamon rolls in one of the warming trays, even though they looked and smelled amazing. He opened the lid to a second warming tray and found sausage links and bacon, and he took several of each. The last warming tray had a quiche cut into small squares, and he took one of those, too. The cold tray contained fresh diced fruit, and Cian hummed in appreciation as he helped himself to some.

Can't remember the last time I had kiwi.

After setting his plate on the table, Cian moved to the coffee service. He poured himself a cup of the dark brew. Cian grabbed silverware and a couple of napkins before returning to the table.

Cian had just settled at his plate when a man and woman entered the room. They were dressed casually in clothes suitable for hiking. The blonde woman flashed a smile at Cian before following the dark-haired man to the counter to fix a plate.

Focusing on his food, Cian ate quickly. He had zero desire to make small talk. Instead, Cian wanted to get the hell out of Dodge.

When the pair sat near the other end of the table, Cian hoped he'd gotten his wish. Unfortunately, he didn't seem to be that lucky. After taking a couple of bites, the woman turned and smiled at him again.

"Hi, I'm Evie," she told him. Tipping her fork at the man next to him, she added, "He's Duke."

Cian swallowed his bite of food and nodded politely. "Cian." He tapped his chest with the tips of two fingers. Glancing over their attire again, Cian went with, "Hiking?"

Evie nodded with a grin. "Yep. There's supposed to be some great scenery around here." Eyeing him speculatively, she asked, "What about you?"

Shaking his head, Cian told her, "No. Just passing through." He pointed at his cane which he'd propped up against the side of the table. "Stopped a couple of days to ease the ol' leg before I move on."

"Oh really?" Duke decided to get in on the conversation. "Is that motorcycle outside yours? It's pretty sweet."

Cian nodded. "It is."

For the rest of the meal, Cian and Duke chatted about motorcycles. He discovered the man had one at home, but they'd driven a *Jeep* for this trip. Evie didn't enjoy sitting on the back for long stretches, so they did shorter rides around home.

Cian responded politely and finished his food as swiftly as etiquette allowed him. "Enjoy your hiking," he offered, rising to his feet.

"Thanks," Evie responded. A gleam of some emotion Cian couldn't pinpoint entered her blue eyes as she added, "We will."

To Cian's ears, Evie made those words sound a little suggestive. He didn't get it. Maybe she intended to get lucky while out on the trail.

Dismissing it, Cian piled his empty mug on his plate. He gripped his cane in his right hand and the plate in his left. Taking everything to a blue plastic tub with a sign over it saying, "Please place dirty dishes here," Cian dropped them off, then returned to his room.

The hairs on the back of his neck stood on end, and he barely resisted glancing over his shoulder at them. After rounding the corner and ensuring he was out of sight, he shook his head. Cian didn't get most people, which was why he liked his secluded acreage so much.

Time to go home.

A few minutes later, Cian was outside tucking his duffel into a saddlebag. He pulled on his leather jacket and picked up his helmet. Before he slipped it over his head, he heard his phone ring.

Cian set it on a handlebar and pulled out his phone. Seeing Tyler's number on the screen, he answered it. He turned, resting his butt on the seat.

"Hi, Tyler," Cian greeted, wondering what his army buddy needed.

"Did you find the place?"

Cian grimaced. He should have realized Tyler would be curious. "I did," he confirmed, wondering how to explain while keeping his promise.

"And? Don't leave me hangin,' man?" His amusement clear in his tone, Tyler asked, "Was your little Praerna everything you hoped he would be? Did you spend all night fuckin'?"

"No, we didn't fuck all night," Cian growled, surprised at how much ire filled him upon hearing Tyler's irreverent comment. Clearing his throat, he told his buddy, "I did meet him, and we discussed why he's such a private person." After a second of hesitation, Cian decided to share, "They weren't what I expected, and they definitely have a different take on religion. It's a little . . . old-school. I can see how others could persecute them if word got out."

"Huh. Okay." The sound of Tyler tapping on keys came through the line. "Do you have to convert in order to stay with your little hottie, then?" Then Tyler chuckled. "Is Praerna a hottie?"

"You know, I'd describe him as . . . cute," Cian admitted, surprised when he realized he truly felt that way. His purple hide had been interesting, but what really had drawn him in was his hair and eyes, not to mention — "He has a very sweet face. Kind, ya know?" Cian shook his head. "That probably doesn't really make sense, but it's something about his eyes. Like he's seen so much shit but still has hope." Frowning at the ground, he murmured, "And he dyes his hair green and wears it in these short spikes." Cian shrugged. "He's damn adorable."

Why am I walking away from that again?

But he's a gargoyle?

And why do I give a shit about that?

"Well, it sounds like you're damn smitten with him," Tyler commented. "And that you're going to see him again today, right?"

"Uhhh . . ."

Tyler didn't wait for Cian to come up with some kind of intelligent answer. "When you see him again, you should have him warn whoever runs security at his commune that there are others searching for them, too," Tyler told him, the sound of his fingers tapping away continuing. "I think they piggybacked off my hack, and you're not going to believe some of the shit they're claiming about that place."

"What are you talking about?" Cian asked, worry filling him. "What kind of shit?"

"The kind of shit that could get them locked up by the people in white coats," Tyler claimed with a snort. "Seriously, listen to this message they sent me yesterday. *There have always been those who commune with demons, and those sorts of devil worshipers must be stamped out for the safety of good folk like you. You should stay far away from them while we eradicate their threat to the world.*"

"Holy shit," Cian whispered. Glancing around quickly, he made certain no other guests were about to possibly overhear his conversation. Fortunately, he was alone. "They contacted you? How? Why?"

"Evidently, they've been trying to figure out Praerna's location, too . . . or someone else from that area. They noticed me looking into the area and sent me an email message titled *Demon Worshipers live near Lake Point.* I almost deleted it without reading it," Tyler stated. He sounded disgusted. "Can you believe that shit? Devil worshipers and demons?" Then Tyler's tone turned musing. "You said they have an old-school religion. Think they're into that?"

"No, absolutely not," Cian countered, even going so far as to shake his head. "Old-school, as in they believe Fate is real and probably some other old-timey gods. I didn't get into specifics."

But if the average person spotted a gargoyle in their true form, they just might think that they were facing a demon.

Shit.

"Do you want me to respond to these guys?" Tyler's question cut into Cian's thoughts. "Maybe see if I can get some more intel on why they think that or what their plans are for taking out these so-called demons?"

Cian hesitated.

Should he get Tyler even more involved?

Plus, Cian knew if he did that, it meant he couldn't go anywhere. He would need to stay to pass along the information. Except, if he walked away without warning them, it was like abandoning the innocent. That wasn't something he could do. Helping and protecting people was one of the main reasons he'd joined the military in the first place.

After taking a deep quiet breath, Cian told his buddy, "If you don't mind. These guys need to be warned."

"Sounds good. I'll keep you posted."

A second later, Tyler disconnected the line.

Cian pulled on his helmet and slung his leg over his motorcycle. Instead of heading east, toward home, he headed west, toward Praerna and his clutch.

CHAPTER SIX

"He came back?"

Praerna stared at Chieftain Kinsey, hope flooding him. When he'd woken from roost, he'd been shocked to see his chieftain sitting on the edge of the roof. Kinsey was cradling a tumbler between his palms, waiting for him to wake.

"Yes, Cian came back this morning," Chieftain Kinsey told him, repeating his claim that Cian was there at the clutch estate. "He did admit that he was intending to return home, but he received troubling information from his friend, Tyler." Grimacing, Kinsey told him, "It seems, we have another wave of hunters after us."

Groaning, Praerna muttered, "Why can't they just leave us alone?" He crossed his arms over his chest. "We've never done anything to them."

Kinsey reached over and squeezed his shoulder. "We'll never understand why some people have so much hate in their hearts." Offering him an encouraging smile, his chieftain added, "And I hope you never do understand that." Kinsey rose to his feet, offering a hand to Praerna. "Come on. Go clean up. We're setting up a meal in one of the smaller lounges. You can sit and chat with Cian there."

Praerna nodded, taking Kinsey's hand and allowing the larger gargoyle to help him to his feet. As he headed toward the roof ledge, he recalled Kinsey's other words. "So Cian didn't plan to come back? It was just because of the hunters?" Disappointment curdled his gut as he whispered, "So he doesn't really want me?"

"You know it's not as simple as that, Praerna," Kinsey warned, pausing on the ledge. He leveled a serious gaze upon him, saying, "Humans need time to process. They like to come about to the whole fated mate thing in their own time. This just sped up his return, that's all."

"So you really think Cian would have returned?" Praerna asked, peering up into his leader's yellowish-orange features.

Kinsey scoffed softly as he smirked. "Well, Fate would have made Cian's life a bitch the longer he resisted." With a shrug, he added, "You know how she likes to get her way." Then Kinsey winked, his green eyes twinkling. "Besides, if he'd been gone for more than a week, we would have taken you to go get him."

Gasping, Praerna gaped at his chieftain. "You'd kidnap him? Bring him here without his permission?"

Shrugging, Kinsey countered, "We would have convinced him of the error of his ways." He patted Praerna's shoulder again before spreading his large white wings. "This is your future, Praerna. Sometimes, securing it takes a little coercion, but it's always worth the extra effort."

Then Kinsey jumped from the ledge.

Praerna watched as his chieftain flapped once before dipping a wing and floating in an arc toward a third-floor balcony. Jimmy waited there, bundled in a blanket and sitting on a swing. After Kinsey landed, the big gargoyle pecked a kiss to Jimmy's lips before picking him up, blanket and all. Kinsey settled on the swing with Jimmy in his lap, and the small human snuggled close.

With a sigh, Praerna turned away from the sweet sight. He spread his arms, lifting his hands over his head. With hardly a thought, he extended his bone-spurs that lay along three of his ribs on either side of his back. The flexible cartilage stretched out the folds of skin that attached under his upper arms and down along his torso.

Praerna jumped from the building's edge. He used his arms to steer as his wingskins billowed around him. With a lowering of his left arm, he veered that way. Praerna landed on a third-story balcony that opened into the hallway of his wing.

As Praerna moved toward the door, he retracted his bone-spurs, causing his wingskins to lie mostly flush to his body. He paused for just a few seconds in the doorway, appreciating the cool evening wind on his cheeks. Then thoughts of his mate waiting for him urged him indoors, and he hurried to his suite.

Fifteen minutes later, Praerna stood outside the lounge Second Destrawn had indicated. The big, dark-green gargoyle had sent him a text while he'd been in the shower. He appreciated the second's forethought, since Praerna had completely forgotten to ask the chieftain.

Nerves filled him, and he shifted his weight from foot to foot. Butterflies bumped in his belly. He knew he was sort of hungry, since he'd just woken, but he wasn't totally certain he would be able to eat anything.

"Just go in, Praerna."

Upon hearing the soft, encouraging voice behind him, Praerna turned and spotted Holden. The gargoyle was a larger one with deep-purple skin and black wings and claws, and he was new to the clutch. He'd bonded with Lathe, a vampire that lived with them and who handled their technology stuff.

Holden smiled at him kindly. "Lathe and I spent some time with Cian during the day," the male revealed. He used the mug of something he held in his right hand to indicate the door. "Cian's a good guy. Honest and straightforward with a deep commitment to honor. When he knew we were about to be targeted by hunters, he couldn't walk away, even though what we are still freaks him out a little." Stepping forward, Holden patted Praerna on his upper back. "Give him a chance to get to know you now that he's had a day to decompress. I think he'll surprise you."

Praerna nodded even as he swallowed hard. "I can do this," he whispered, more to himself than to Holden.

Still, Holden grinned broadly. "You can do this."

With a sharp nod, Praerna turned back to face the door. He knocked lightly, warning whoever was on the other side — just in case Cian wasn't alone — that someone was entering. Then Praerna opened the door and eased into the room.

Praerna paused just inside, closing the door softly behind him. He quickly took in the romantic dinner for two set up on the coffee table. Someone had even lit a pair of candlesticks. Two plates, still covered, had been placed near each other with cushions before them, obviously to sit on. The only thing Praerna didn't see were drinks, but that was fine. The lounge boasted a fully stocked bar as well as a couple of carafes that probably contained coffee or juice or something similar.

"They really went all out, didn't they?"

Hearing Cian's soft tenor, Praerna snapped his attention to the left. He saw his human exiting the attached bathroom. He gripped his cane in his right hand as he slowly limped forward. His dark-eyed gaze roved over Praerna's form even as they narrowed just a little.

Praerna had no idea how to interpret the human's gaze. He'd had very little one-on-one interaction with humans. Under Chieftain Grecian, no one had found their mates. There had been only a handful of humans in the clutch when he'd taken over. Praerna was friends with them, but since they were mates of other gargoyles, he wasn't *that* friendly with them.

Now, however, he had to figure out how to talk to a complete stranger and a human to boot.

"Um, yeah," Praerna responded, mentally cringing at how inane he sounded. Wrapping his arms around his torso, he glanced toward the coffee table once more. "They do that."

Cian lifted his free hand and swept it toward the table. "Shall we sit and eat, then?" He took a step in that direction. "It smells good, and they told me gargoyles are normally hungry after waking from . . . roost." Cian hesitated a second before asking, "Is that the right word?"

Praerna nodded. "It is. When we sleep in stone form, we call it roost." He started toward the sideboard, needing water to help his dry mouth. "Um, r-roosting, I guess."

A low chuckle escaped Cian. "Roosting. Okay." He followed Praerna toward the drinks. "They certainly offer quite the variety."

Nodding again, Praerna started to feel a little like a bobblehead. "Yeah." He forced himself to turn and focus on Cian, which really wasn't a hardship. After all, his human was a handsome man, and he smelled amazing. "So what can I get you?" As Praerna spoke, he watched Cian draw closer, his chin tipping up and up. "Oh, you're taller than I thought."

Cian arched one brow as he paused next to him. "Is that a bad thing?"

"No, no!" Praerna cried, quickly shaking his head. He lifted a hand, intending to touch his human's shirt-clad chest. Just as quickly, he hesitated, uncertain, and lowered his hand. "Um, I was just surprised. That's all." Smiling, Praerna peered at him through his lashes. "Pleased, too. Um, I like your height." He shrugged. "Maybe because I'm pretty short."

Praerna only stood five-foot-eight, and he knew that many considered that short, even for a human. Large gargoyles stood upward of six-foot-six and more. Second Destrawn nearly topped seven feet.

"I'm glad you don't mind," Cian murmured, sounding awkward. He glanced toward the offered beverages while clearing his throat. "Well, uh . . . I don't want caffeine. Too late for me." Cutting a side-eyed look Praerna's way, Cian added, "You okay if I have a rum and decaf coke?"

"Sure," Praerna replied, uncertain why Cian would think he needed permission. "I don't mind." He even bent and began rummaging in the mini-fridge placed under the bar. Grabbing a can, Praerna held it up. "Um, it's *Pepsi* brand. Is that okay?"

Cian nodded. "Sure. I don't really have a preference."

Praerna smiled as he popped the top. "I'll let you make it first, and I can watch to see how much you mix of each." Seeing Cian lift a black eyebrow in silent question, Praerna explained, "That way, I'll know for the future."

"Okay."

As Praerna scented each of the carafes, checking their contents, he watched Cian pour his drink. He noted the alcohol-to-soda ratio his human favored. Praerna tucked that information away as he poured himself a glass of orange juice.

"Not a fan of coffee?" Cian asked, curiosity in his tone.

Shaking his head, Praerna admitted, "When we were ruled by Chieftain Grecian, the wingless gargoyles weren't allowed coffee." He shrugged as he started toward the coffee table. "Some of my friends really missed it, but I could take or leave it. When we were allowed coffee again, I never really reacquired the taste, so I just don't bother."

Cian's eyes narrowed even as he fell into step beside him, limping a little on his right leg, even with the cane. "Wingless gargoyles." He swept his gaze over Praerna's form. "Not like your larger brethren who have the massive wings. Does that mean you can't fly?"

Praerna smiled up at Cian. "Oh, no. I can fly. It's just different." He placed his drink next to a covered plate.

"How?" Cian placed his tumbler on the table, too, before straightening and adding, "If you don't mind me asking."

"Oh, I don't mind." Praerna lifted his arms, showing off the folds of extra skin lying against his body. "I have wingskins." Then Praerna partly turned his back to his mate. "And bone-spurs."

With a thought, Praerna extended his bone-spurs, causing his wingskins to stretch out to either side of his torso.

"Damn," Cian whispered, surprise filling his tone and scent. "That's amazing."

Praerna felt a measure of relief when he realized he didn't scent any disgust or disbelief from Cian. Instead, his mate smelled of interest. A few seconds later, Praerna felt a soft touch to his right wingskin, and he sucked in a shocked gasp as arousal sizzled through his veins. He almost missed Cian's next whispered comment.

"And you can fly with these?"

On instinct, Praerna snapped his bone-spurs in and dropped his arms, slapping his wingskins back against his body. He gasped and spun. Taking in Cian's wide-eyed look of shock, not to mention how he'd lifted his hands in placation—his cane dangling from his right hand—Praerna realized how odd that knee-jerk reaction would be to an unknowing human.

Still, Praerna couldn't have helped it even if he'd tried.

"Whoa, sorry." Cian kept his voice soft and low, soothing. He even took a halting step backward. "I didn't mean to offend. Should I, uh . . . so touching wings are a no-no?"

Praerna jerked a nod even as he tried to get his suddenly raging libido under control. He couldn't remember the last time he'd been turned on so fast and so hard. His prick ached behind his loincloth, and he knew that if he looked down, he would see it tented obscenely.

He didn't look, though.

Instead, Praerna's need to soothe his clearly upset mate kicked into overdrive.

Praerna lifted his own hands, palms out. Unfortunately, that only caused Cian to take another step backward.

Damn it.

"It is, but not for you," Praerna blurted, struggling to get his mate to understand. "You can touch anywhere on me. I just wasn't expecting it. Ha. Ha." His bark of laughter came out a little high, even to his own ears. Praerna tried to take a deep breath, but he still didn't feel like he'd gotten enough air into his lungs. "Wings and tails are special. You don't touch without permission. They're incredibly sensitive."

"Wings and tails?" Cian appeared to be calming down, lowering his cane back to the floor. Some of the tension in his shoulders eased. "Okay." His gaze flitted down to where Praerna had his own tail wrapped around his left thigh. "No touching wings or tails." Frowning, Cian cocked his head. "Sensitive how? And why not for me?"

"For you with me. Um, only me." When Cian's scent flooded with confusion, Praerna realized he wasn't making sense. Tipping his head back, he growled, "Ugh! It's so hard to talk to you when I've never been so horny in my life." Huffing a breath, Praerna dropped onto the pillow before his plate, then scrubbed his fingers through his hair, tugging at his stiff locks. "Maybe if we focus on eating, I can string a few sentences together." Grabbing his orange juice, he took a long, deep drink.

For a few seconds, Cian didn't move.

As Praerna set his glass back on the table, he peered up at Cian. He spotted the dark-haired human's wide eyes and slightly parted lips. Then where his mate's attention was focused registered to Praerna.

My loincloth.

Praerna glanced down, saw the expected tenting, and felt heat bloom under the surface of his hide for a whole new reason. Nibbling his bottom lip, he peered at Cian from beneath his lashes. Praerna had no idea what to say . . . except . . .

"Sorry," Praerna whispered. "C-Can't help it."

"I know you're attracted to me," Cian began softly, resting his cane against the sofa at their back. "But *that* attracted?" He seemed shocked as he began easing his butt onto the cushion. "How is that possible?"

Seeing Cian's wince as he settled to the floor, his butt on the pillow, Praerna realized he really should have second-guessed the seating.

"Are you okay?" Praerna asked quickly, reaching out to touch Cian's upper arm. "We can move to the sofa. I can get TV trays." He began scrambling to his feet. "We don't have to sit on the floor if it hurts you."

"No, stop." Cian grabbed Praerna's upper arm, staying his movement and keeping him on his pillow. "Now that I'm down here, it's fine." Then Cian offered him a rueful smile. "I may need a hand standing back up again, though."

Praerna nodded eagerly, enjoying the feel of Cian's warm palm against his arm. "Okay."

Anything for my mate.

CHAPTER SEVEN

Cian found himself touched by Praerna's eagerness to please. He'd never had a date, lover, anyone, who watched his cues so attentively. Praerna not only wanted to know exactly how Cian made his drink, but the second it looked like sitting on the floor wasn't comfortable, he began throwing out alternatives.

Damn. That's . . . really nice.

While it didn't take any stretch of Cian's nearly nonexistent imagination to realize that he would end up being the dominant in their relationship, that didn't mean Praerna would be a pushover, either.

And damn, guess I'm accepting this relationship. Just had to get my head around the whole gargoyle thing.

"So what did we end up with?" Cian asked as he lifted the lid from his plate. He hummed as he eyed the steak, lobster tail, and mashed potatoes. "Surf and turf. Nice."

Cian was damn glad he wasn't allergic to shellfish.

"Oh, wow." Praerna stared at his plate with wide yellow eyes. "I don't think I've ever had lobster."

"No?" Cian tucked his napkin into the collar of his shirt before picking up his knife and fork. "Never in all your, what, couple of hundred years?"

That was something Cian was still wrapping his brain around. Bonding with a gargoyle meant prospectively living for centuries—centuries upon centuries, in fact. While most paranormals lived upward of five hundred years, a gargoyle had the rare nature of existing for a couple of thousand.

No wonder mates are so important to paranormals. That'd be a long life alone.

"I'm considered fairly young for a gargoyle," Praerna revealed, tucking into his own meal. "I don't know my exact birthdate, but I've lived one hundred eighty-three summers."

"Wow." Cian cut into his food, glancing at the cute, pale purple male seated next to him. "That's still impressive to me."

Praerna beamed a smile at him, then answered his other question. "And no. For a long time, this clutch was ruled by an asshole." Waving his fork to indicate himself, Praerna told him, "Wingless gargoyles like me were treated like second-class citizens. We did the menial, manual labor tasks, like cooking, cleaning, and laundry, while the winged gargoyles led and handled security." Praerna shrugged. "We weren't allowed these types of expensive foods. They were reserved for the inner circle when they had meetings with others." Scoffing, he added, "And we sure as hell wouldn't have been allowed to spend money on online games or a gaming system."

Cian frowned as he chewed his bite of perfectly grilled steak. "Damn," he muttered around his mouthful of meat before swallowing. "Glad that asshole isn't in charge anymore." *Or we never would have met.* Keeping that thought to himself, Cian asked, "What happened to him?"

"After Chieftain Kinsey won in a Right for Position challenge, unseating his power, he was taken away by the elder and his guards." As Praerna spoke, he began carefully pulling the lobster meat from the tail. "Elder Vermidian came back last year and reported that Grecian had been put down due to his crimes against our kind."

Nodding, Cian murmured, "Does that sort of thing happen often?"

From Praerna's flat tone as he'd shared the tale, he could read between the lines. The gargoyle certainly wasn't sorry to see him gone. Cian didn't blame him one little bit.

Praerna met Cian's gaze as he shook his head. "No. There aren't nearly as many gargoyles as there are other paranormals," he explained. "The circle of elders uses termination as a last resort. They try rehabilitation first, but Grecian refused to change, so they didn't have a choice."

"Then that's on him." Cian decided it was time for a new topic. "Have you created any new topiaries recently?"

Grinning, Praerna nodded as he popped a bite of lobster into his mouth. His eyes widened as he chewed. A low, appreciative moan escaped him, and he even closed his eyes.

Cian felt his blood heat in his veins, pooling in his groin. While the other gargoyles had explained that the mate-pull didn't force him to be attracted to Praerna—he would have been attracted to the gargoyle anyway—they had told him that it did ramp up his arousal. Cian just hadn't expected it to happen to him so swiftly.

Except, damn, the noises Praerna is making.

As Cian stared in shock, arousal simmering through him, Praerna kept eating his lobster, muttering about how good it was. The appreciative noises made it sound almost as if the little gargoyle was making love to the food. It was damn near obscene, and Cian couldn't stop his visceral reaction.

Wow!

Finally, when the lobster tail was gone, Praerna took a breath and peered up at him. "Do you not like yours?" He glanced at it with a hopeful gleam in his eyes.

"Uh, yeah. I do," Cian managed to mutter after a swift, hard swallow. "Everything is excellent." He stabbed his fork into his garlic mashed potatoes, wondering if he could survive another round of that if he offered Praerna his lobster tail. "Uh, just got caught up in listening to you enjoying yours." Unable to resist, no matter how uncomfortable it would make his jeans, Cian indicated his plate. "You can have mine, if you want."

Praerna shook his head. "Oh, no. I couldn't do that." Before

Cian could insist that he didn't mind, the gargoyle reached for the lid of another plate — one the size of a serving platter — that had been left on the coffee table. It rested a little further away from them, halfway between them. "I wonder if this is dessert."

Before Cian could tell Praerna that Sorbin had put a box in the fridge and had told him it was dessert, Praerna lifted the lid and let out an excited squeal. Cian couldn't help but grin. On the platter were two more lobster tails along with another pair of steaks. A heaping dollop of mashed potatoes rested in the middle.

"Holy shit," Cian whispered, watching Praerna take another lobster tail, practically dancing on his seat cushion. "How could they possibly expect us to eat all this?"

As Praerna tore into the fresh lobster tail, he told him, "In general, paranormals eat quite a bit more than the average human." He paused in cutting the lobster meat to grin at him. "Although, I think they forgot that I'm a small gargoyle and don't eat quite as much as they would."

Cian pointed at the cup of melted butter on Praerna's plate. "That's to dip the lobster in." He'd noticed the gargoyle hadn't used it on the first tail, and since the male had told him he'd never had lobster before, it occurred to him that Praerna may not have known.

"Oh, right." Praerna chuckled softly, ducking his head in what looked like embarrassment. "I forgot."

Reaching over, Cian rested his hand on Praerna's back. He rubbed up and down the spine lightly, hoping to relax him. "I wasn't certain if you were aware," he explained, finding the slightly bumpy hide under his fingers fascinating. "Not everyone uses it. I like it both ways."

To prove his point, Cian dipped a hunk of lobster meat into the little cup of butter on his own plate. He popped the tasty morsel into his mouth. Unable to resist, Cian let out his own hum of pleasure.

Cian couldn't remember the last time he'd had lobster, and it really was good.

"Oh, you sound like you enjoy that," Praerna whispered, staring at him with wide eyes. He even swayed closer a little while sniffing, and he glanced at Cian's crotch before straightening and murmuring, "Oh," again.

Chuckling as he swallowed, Cian winked at the smaller male. "Now you know why I was staring." A low growl entered his voice as he admitted, "The noises you were making, the proof of your enjoyment of trying a food you'd been denied, well . . . it was incredibly . . . arousing."

Considering Cian had been told that paranormals—and gargoyles especially—had a heightened sense of smell, there was no point in trying to be coy about it. He was aroused as hell. There was no way that Praerna would have missed the way Cian was tenting his fly with his aching erection.

"I-I did that t-to you?"

Cian nearly groaned upon hearing Praerna's breathy question. "Yes, Praerna," he responded roughly. Deciding to continue being straightforward, Cian curved his lips into a hungry smile as he held the gargoyle's gaze. "I was almost half in love with you before even meeting you. Losing contact with you drove me nuts." Cian saw the way Praerna nibbled his bottom lip, and he wondered what the male's mouth would feel like against his own, what he would taste like. *Probably sweet like the lobster.* Trying to keep control of himself, Cian continued, "I felt compelled to find you. The mate-pull explains part of that, and I admit, I was thrown for a loop with the whole gargoyle thing." Scoffing, Cian admitted, "I don't have much of an imagination, so I never would have dreamed of this." Finally, realizing he was rambling, Cian forced his thoughts in order so he could get to the point. "I heard your voice before I saw you, and it turned me on. Yes, the fact that you're a gargoyle threw me, but this between us, I wanted you when I thought you were some disfigured human. That you're a sexy-as-hell gargoyle, well . . . that doesn't change my desire."

By the time Cian stopped his verbal diarrhea, Praerna was smiling widely, joy filling his eyes. The yellow orbs appeared to gleam with anticipation, broken by the vertical slit of his pupil, which appeared to be more dilated than before. His nostrils were flared, and his chest lifted and fell in swift panting breaths. There even appeared to be a pinkish flush beginning to darken the light-purple skin of his neck and upper torso.

Absolutely stunning.

Damn, I want to lick every inch of that blush.

"You think I'm sexy-as-hell?" Praerna whispered before nibbling his bottom lip. "And you want to be with me? Really?"

"Yes to both, Praerna."

Cian began leaning toward the smaller male, intending to satisfy his curiosity about how Praerna would taste. Except, Cian's stomach took that moment to rumble, reminding him that he'd only had a few bites of dinner. When Praerna's stomach talked, seeming to answer his own, Cian chuckled and straightened.

"Okay. I think it's time we both finish dinner." Cian picked up his rum and soda, searching for something to cool his heated flesh. As he pressed the chilly tumbler against his temple, he smirked at Praerna. "We'll pick this up after we've filled our bellies."

Praerna groaned even as he nodded. "Yeah." As he stabbed a bite of steak, he flashed a hungry look Cian's way. "After all, you'll need your strength for what I want to do to you."

"Same," Cian rumbled before taking a sip of his drink. The decaf soda mellowed the harsh tang of the rum, and he took a deeper swallow. Setting his drink down, Cian grabbed his fork as he waggled his eyebrows. "I'd say eat fast, but rushing this delicious meal would be an absolute crime."

Barking a laugh, Praerna nodded. Then he took another bite of the lobster.

Racking his brain for a safe topic, Cian returned to an earlier thought. "Have you created any new topiaries recently?" He'd missed reading the enthusiasm in Praerna's words when he'd chatted about them.

Immediately, Praerna grinned as he nodded and chewed. Once he'd swallowed, he claimed, "I've been watching *YouTube* videos about different techniques." As Praerna scooped up a healthy dollop of mashed potatoes, he told him, "I made a southern lady with a parasol. The guys got a kick out of it."

"Like the one *Brendan Frasier* made in the *Dudley Do-Right* movie?" Cian recalled the cute film.

Praerna swallowed his mashed potatoes while shaking his head. "I don't know that one."

"We'll watch it," Cian declared. He enjoyed the light-hearted movie. "He makes it with a chainsaw."

Grinning, Praerna nodded eagerly. "Okay. That sounds cool."

"It's a date," Cian declared with a grin before popping a bite of lobster into his mouth. "Damn. That really is good," he muttered with a hum. Pointing at it, Cian asked, "Why would your clutch even have lobster on hand?"

"Kinsey's mother is coming here in a couple of days," Praerna revealed. "Jimmy is getting close to his due date, and she wants to be here for the laying."

Cian froze, cocking his head. "Uh, what?" Seeing Praerna's eyes widen, he realized he must have missed something. "I think there was a gap in the explanations somewhere. Can you explain that statement?"

As Cian watched Praerna's mouth open, then close, he took

a bite of mashed potatoes. "Is it that bad?" he asked, seeing the worry filling Praerna's eyes.

"Um, no." Praerna's voice squeaked, belying his words. "N-Not really."

Sighing, Cian worried he didn't want to know. He'd already had so much information dumped on him. Considering his lack of imagination, he couldn't fathom what else there could be.

"Better just get it out there, Praerna," Cian encouraged softly as he cut off a bite of his steak. Before popping it into his mouth, he guessed, "From your reaction, I imagine it's sort of important."

"It is." Praerna's head nodded swiftly. "Very important." Blowing out a breath, he winced. "Human men can find it scary, and I don't want you to change your mind about bonding with me."

Well, that's not troublesome at all.

Cian set his knife down, having cut the last of his meat. "Just tell me, Praerna," he encouraged, gripping his wrist in a light hold and squeezing gently. "I can't deal with it if I don't know."

Praerna jerked a sharp nod. "Right." His expression turned firm. "Okay, so, I guess what was missed is that a gargoyle, once bonded with their fated male mate, can impregnate said male mate."

Rolling those words around in his head, Cian felt certain he was misunderstanding. "Come again?"

"Jimmy is a human male, he's Kinsey's fated mate, and he's pregnant." Praerna's short, blunt sentences might have sounded rude if they weren't so very necessary. "Kinsey's mother is Wendy, and she's coming here to be with them when Jimmy goes through labor to lay the egg."

Cian eased his grip on Praerna's wrist, and it dropped to his lap. Even his fork fell to the coffee table as his right hand went lax. Frowning at the wall, Cian felt his mind sort of fritz out as he processed those words.

Blurting out the biggest take-away, Cian shook his head in disbelief. "After we bond, you can get me pregnant?"

Praerna nibbled his bottom lip as he nodded, worry etched on his pale purple features. "Yes."

Cian swallowed hard upon hearing the whispered confirmation. "Holy shit."

He had the sudden desire to cross his legs. He wasn't much of a switch, but he did enjoy a nice hard fuck on occasion. Considering the gargoyle had increased strength, even though he was smaller than him, Cian thought he would get it on occasion.

Now, not.

"S-Sooooo . . . after we bond," Cian stated slowly. "You won't be able to fuck me without protection?"

That would suck, too.

Cian had paid attention when Destrawn and Sorbin had explained about paranormals not being able to give or get human diseases—not that he had anything, anyway.

"Well, there's an easy spermicide for a gargoyle," Praerna told him softly. "Cinnamon renders us infertile. Regardless of which of us eats it."

"Damn." Cian scoffed, shaking his head. "Now I wish I'd eaten that cinnamon roll for breakfast."

CHAPTER EIGHT

Praerna didn't know what cinnamon roll Cian was referring to, but he silently agreed. "A lot of guys eat cinnamon rolls or cinnamon toast every morning," he admitted. Rubbing the back of his neck, he glanced over their food. "Huh. Usually, they always offer something with cinnamon to a new couple."

Cian pointed at the mini-fridge. "Sorbin put a carton in there. Not sure what's in it." Rolling one shoulder in a half-shrug, Cian stated, "Said it was dessert and told us not to forget it."

Rising to his feet, Praerna hurried over there. He opened the door and spotted a cardboard carton. Once he'd grabbed it, Praerna returned to the coffee table and retook his seat.

Using the box, Praerna pushed his plate out of the way. He opened it and peered inside. With a soft gasp, he pulled out the delicious-looking item.

"Coffee cake with icing," Praerna murmured reverently, his mouth watering even after all he'd eaten. "I bet it's Jimmy's recipe. He hasn't made it since before he decided to get pregnant."

"A cake heavy with cinnamon," Cian rumbled, nodding. "Very nice. You seem pretty excited about it." He smirked at Praerna as he held up his knife. "But a whole bunt cake just for us?" Cian picked up his knife and wiped his napkin over it. "Or are we supposed to leave the leftovers in the fridge?"

Praerna chuckled as he quickly shook his head. "I'm not leaving the leftovers," he declared. Seeing the amused curve of Cian's lips, he stated, "I'm claiming this as a congratulations gift for finding my mate."

Barking a laugh, Cian nodded. "That good, huh?"

Nodding, Praerna watched as Cian cut into the cake, slicing off a healthy-sized piece. "Jimmy used to get special requests, but with his pregnancy progressing, he started having trouble with the smell of baked foods, so he stopped making it." A wealth of pleasure flooded Praerna, realizing the chieftain's mate had overcome his discomfort to make the cake for him. "This is all ours."

"I can't wait to try it," Cian stated, placing the piece on Praerna's plate. "It smells delicious, even cold."

Praerna watched Cian cut a smaller piece for himself. His human smiled when he caught Praerna's questioning look. Cian chuckled as he settled the chunk onto his own plate.

"I'm quite full, but I understand the importance of the gift," Cian told him, setting down the knife so he could pick up his fork again. "Plus, even full, my mouth is watering for a bite, but I can't eat as much as I'm guessing you as a gargoyle can."

Nodding in understanding, Praerna stabbed his fork into the baked treat. His mouth watered in anticipation as he brought it to his lips. After easing the forkful into his mouth, Praerna moaned softly as the flavor of the cake exploded across his taste buds.

"Better than I remember," Praerna mumbled after swallowing. As he gathered another forkful, he commented, "Must be because I haven't had it in a while."

Cian grunted softly, nodding. "Yeah. That's good." While lifting more to his mouth, he admitted, "Can't remember the last time I had coffee cake. I live alone and don't make baked goods. Too much sugar."

"You don't like things with sugar?" Praerna realized they'd never discussed food preferences before. "I bet you take your coffee black."

"You'd be right. Most of the time, I do," Cian replied with a nod. "And it's not that I don't like them. It's that I have to have them in moderation." He patted his flat stomach. "I have to work hard to stay in shape. Otherwise, what's left of my thigh muscle isn't going to be able to support me." With a shrug, Cian told him, "Being overweight just wouldn't work for me."

As Praerna nodded, he commented, "Well, you shouldn't have to worry about that in the future."

"No?"

Hearing the silent question behind the single word, Praerna smiled shyly at him. "Yeah. Your aging will slow to match mine, your bones and muscles will grow stronger, and your health and immunities will improve."

Cian nodded. "I recall that being touched on, now that you mention it. Nice perks."

Praerna grinned, silently agreeing. He continued eating his cake, keeping his mouth full because it was just that good.

After a few moments of eating in silence, Cian swallowed and told him, "But you know that's not why I agreed to bond with you, right?"

After a second of hesitation, Praerna nodded. "You already told me you wanted me even before you came here." He batted his eyelashes at Cian. "And you think I'm sexy-as-sin."

Chuckling, Cian nodded. "Exactly." He set his fork on his freshly emptied plate and picked up his tumbler. "So." Leaning back against the sofa behind him, Cian watched Praerna as he continued to eat. "When I thought about finding and winning a partner, I always assumed I'd take him or her out on dates to learn about them." With a chuckle, Cian pointed out, "But we've been dating for six months without even realizing it."

Praerna ate the last bite of his cake as he thought about that. After swallowing, he beamed at Cian. "We have been, huh?"

Cian downed the last of his drink. "Yes," he answered firmly. Pinning a serious gaze on Praerna, Cian surprised him by saying, "And I hear that paranormals are jealous creatures, so I wanted you to know that the only thing I've been friendly with in all that time is my right hand."

Praerna had just enough presence of mind to swallow before he choked on his last bite of coffee cake. Still, he coughed—once, twice. Grabbing his orange juice, Praerna took a couple of deep swallows.

Once Praerna felt in control, he couldn't help but gape at Cian. "Really?" The word came out a little raspy. He roved his gaze over Cian's handsome face, tanned aristocratic features, and broad shoulders. "Are people where you live blind?" When Praerna saw Cian's right black eyebrow lift just a smidge, coupled with an upward quirk of his lips, Praerna had to scoff as he waved his hand up and down in his human's body's general direction. "Come on. You have to know you look amazing. I may be attracted more by scent than by looks, but that doesn't mean I'm stupid. Surely you had to have been beating them off with a stick."

Chuckling softly, Cian smiled warmly at him. He leaned forward and set down his empty glass. Then, to Praerna's surprise, Cian reached for him.

Cian didn't ask permission. He gripped Praerna's near upper arm in a light grasp. Reaching across him, Cian settled his right hand on Praerna's opposite hip. He used the hold to slide him closer, until he was flush to Cian's side, and his human wrapped his closer arm around his back to tuck him against his side.

Praerna was more than happy to cuddle into his human's side.

"Much better," Cian muttered, moving his hand from Praerna's hip. With the backs of his fingers, he skimmed up Praerna's torso. Cian used his thumb to flick Praerna's beaded nipple as he passed it by, drawing a shaky hiss from Praerna, until Cian cradled Praerna's jaw. Using the other to tip Praerna's chin up, Cian peered into his eyes as he said, "Sure, I've had a few second looks while I've been out with my army buddies. Even the cane doesn't scare them all off." His eyes narrowed, and his tone turned husky. "But I'm *picky*."

Smiling shyly up at Cian, Praerna murmured, "You must have been waiting for a guy with purple skin, green hair, yellow eyes, and knows how to fly." Seeing the way Cian's lips curved even wider, Praerna felt a measure of boldness fill him, and he added, "And one you think is sexy-as-sin, of course."

"Yes, Praerna," Cian rumbled, a low husky chuckle filling his words. "Yes, that's exactly right."

Then Cian lowered his head and sealed his lips over Praerna's.

Praerna was so surprised by the kiss, he gasped.

Cian took complete advantage. He eased his tongue a little way into Praerna's mouth, touching the tips of their appendages together. Then he slid them side by side, rubbing sensually, before he began to back off.

Tilting his head a bit, Praerna chased after him. He didn't want the exquisite teasing to end. Praerna wanted more.

Praerna lifted his hand and gripped Cian's forearm. He slipped his other arm around his human's back, clutching at him. Pushing forward, Praerna slid his tongue into Cian's mouth and began doing a little tasting and teasing of his own.

Cian's masculine flavor exploded across his tongue. His mate tasted a little sweet from the coffee cake, coupled with tones of bitterness from the rum. As Praerna pushed his long tongue further into his mouth, something deeper and masculine exploded across his sensitive taste buds, something that brought a primitive thrill to Praerna.

In his mind, Praerna couldn't help but chant — *mine, mine,*

mine.

This was his human, his mate, the other half of his soul. The fact that he'd been talking with him for months, that he felt as if he knew him already when they'd met, had shocked him. Having his mate initiate holding him and kissing him just about damn near blew his mind.

Gods, my mate is perfect.

Cian kissed him back, keeping the kiss slow and sensual. After lapping at his tongue, he suckled the appendage lightly. Feeding Cian a moan, Praerna felt tingles spread down his chest, and his already beaded nipples ached pleasantly.

Easing the kiss to an end, nipping Praerna's bottom lip in the process, Cian pinned him with a hungry smile.

"You taste fantastic, Praerna," Cian rumbled with a feral-looking smile. Then he cocked his head to the side a bit and added, "And your tongue feels longer than I expected it would."

Hearing Cian's absent comment, Praerna couldn't help but grin. "That's because it is longer than a human's. Longer and narrower." Waggling his brows, he added, "With loads more sensory receptors on it, all the better to taste you with."

Cian's black brows shot up. "Huh." Scoffing sharply, he muttered, "I'll have to always remember to brush my teeth before bed." When Praerna gaped, not following, Cian shrugged one shoulder. "I've heard morning breath can be a bad thing. Don't want to wake up tasting bad unless I'm sick or something."

"Huh. Never thought of that." A slow burn of jealousy churned in his gut, fighting with his arousal. "You wake up with others often?" Grimacing, he quickly shook his head, lowering his gaze to the coffee table. "Ugh. Don't answer that. You just told me you hadn't done anything with anyone in over six months. Sorry."

"Hey, I already told you I knew paranormals were jealous." Cian sounded so very understanding as he used his thumb to urge Praerna to meet his gaze once more. "That's why I brought it up. To ease any of your worries." Grimacing, Cian narrowed his eyes as he muttered, "And I'm not going to ask about your sex life. Until we met, whatever it was is really none of my business."

Praerna could scent just a few hints of jealousy wafting from Cian, even though his human seemed to be fighting it. Deciding to put his sweet mate out of his misery, he smiled up at him. When Cian's eyes narrowed a smidge, Praerna eased up to his knees.

"Can I sit on your lap?" Praerna didn't know where his boldness came from, but he started to swing his leg over even before Cian had begun to nod. "Thanks."

A ripple of pleasure washed through him when Cian settled his hands on his hips, just above his loincloth. His skin warmed under his mate's touch. The flesh of his inner thighs tingled as he settled against the fabric of Cian's jeans.

Holding Cian's gaze, Praerna murmured, "I haven't been with anyone in . . . a couple of years." He shrugged, admitting, "Under Chieftain Grecian, it was hard to feel safe enough to get close to someone like that. When Chieftain Kinsey took over, there was so much change and so many new things I was allowed to learn that I had so much else to occupy me." Praerna rubbed his palms down Cian's shoulders, admiring the strength he could feel, even through the shirt. "Now, I'm glad I can end my dry spell with you. My mate."

"I'm a possessive enough bastard to admit that I like that," Cian rumbled, his voice deepening. Tightening his hold, he pulled Praerna's groin flush against his own, blatantly showing off his state of need. "I prefer a bed, cutie. Wanna take me to your suite?"

Feeling Cian's hard erection pressing against his own, Praerna groaned softly and rolled his hips. He reveled in the pressure, and heat erupted through his groin. His cock twitched, aching with need.

"D-Don't wanna move," Praerna whined. "L-Like this t-too much. So good."

Cian growled, his lips peeling away from his teeth in a feral expression. While he tightened his hold on Praerna's hips, he didn't stop him from continuing to rock. Instead, Cian pushed back against the sofa and pressed into his rolling grinds.

"Fuck, Praer," Cian snarled. "You're so fucking right. So good." Then he groaned and shook his head. "Not comin' in my pants, though," Cian declared as he released Praerna's hips.

Praerna froze, thinking perhaps Cian would insist on moving after all, and disappointment filled him.

Then it was Praerna's turn to moan when Cian reached between them and blatantly cupped his erection. His mate squeezed him through his loincloth. Holding his gaze, Cian grinned as, for a few heartbeats, he worked him.

"It looks fairly easy to take this off," Cian commented, gripping the stays on one side with his other hand. "May I?"

"Yes, please," Praerna damn near begged.

Cian didn't ask twice. As he pulled the ties on one side, he released Praerna's dick to do the same on his other. Praerna rose up on his knees, giving his human room to pull the fabric from his body.

"Such a pretty purple prick," Cian murmured, eyeing him as he tossed the loincloth aside. "Long and slender. Beautiful."

Before Praerna's lust-fogged brain could come up with some answer, Cian reached for his fly. He quickly unbuttoned and unzipped his jeans. With a grunt and a hiss, Cian lifted his hips and pushed his jeans and underwear down enough to release his cock.

Praerna gasped at the gorgeous sight before him. His mate's long, hard erection was a thing of beauty. He had a thick girth, his flesh was a deep tan with a reddish hue, and it had to be nearly a foot long.

"I'll be gentle, Praerna," Cian assured, rubbing up and down his back lightly. "You'll be well prepped before I take you."

Realizing his mate misunderstood his silence, Praerna snapped his focus to his face. "You're gorgeous," he whispered before glancing back at Cian's dick. Reaching for his erection, Praerna wrapped his fingers around the thick shaft. "Can't wait to feel this inside me." Hearing Cian groan, he returned his attention to his mate's face. He smiled upon seeing the hungry desire in his dark eyes and the flush to his cheeks and neck. "It'll be perfect."

Clamping one hand onto Praerna's hip, Cian wrapped his other around his erection.

Praerna groaned upon feeling the exquisite squeeze of his mate's hand. When his mate began jacking him, he shuddered at feeling the callouses. His human's slightly roughened palm sent the perfect amount of sensation through his stalk, and it went straight to his balls.

"C-Cian," Praerna whimpered, realizing he was damn close to blowing just from a few strokes.

"Yeah, come for me, Praer," Cian encouraged.

As Cian spoke, he moved his hand to encompass both their cocks. His fingers encouraged Praerna to start moving, too. He took the hint and gripped them both, same as Cian was doing, and began a swift jacking.

Praerna moaned, rutting wantonly into their combined hold. Shudders racked him, and he held onto Cian's shoulder with his other hand for balance. His groin heated further, and his balls pulled tight.

Just as Cian let out a deep sound of pleasure, Praerna felt his own release hit him. Ecstasy lit up his nerve endings as his cock pulsed, splattering bursts of his seed between them.

Groaning Cian's name, Praerna swayed, the bliss sending his senses soaring.

As Praerna continued to tremble, floating happily, he slumped against Cian. He breathed in his new and forever lover's masculine scent, ever-so-pleased to smell his cum, too, telling Praerna that Cian had also come. For a second, when Cian eased his hand out from between them, he worried his human would set him aside now that the passion was over.

Praerna sighed, happiness filling him anew when Cian wrapped his arms around him and cuddled him close.

"So damn perfect, Praerna," Cian whispered into his ear before suckling lightly on the pointed tip. "You're simply amazing."

Smiling, Praerna murmured back, "I'm pretty sure you're the perfect one."

Hearing Cian chuckle, feeling his human's chest rise and fall with the movement, Praerna grinned.

CHAPTER NINE

Cian felt loath to release his hold on the sweet, sexy man curled up on his lap, but he knew he needed to. His butt was beginning to fall asleep, even with the cushion. Also, his thigh was expressing its fair share of discomfort, a dull ache pulsing through him.

After kissing Praerna's temple, Cian murmured into his ear, "I'm sorry, cutie, but I need to get up."

Praerna lifted his head, his smile appearing beautiful on his pale purple features. "Okay," he responded simply. As Praerna eased away from Cian, he snickered softly. "Sorry about your shirt."

Cian took in the cum-splattered fabric and chuckled. "It's fine. It'll wash."

Holding Praerna's hips, Cian helped the gargoyle to his feet. He leaned forward and gripped the hem of his shirt. After whipping the fabric over his head, he lowered it to his groin and cleaned himself up as best he could. Then Cian held it out to Praerna.

"Wanna wipe down with it?" Cian offered. "There's water in the fridge, too, come to think of it."

Praerna took the offered shirt with a shy smile. "This will make me smell like you," he told him as he used a clean corner to wipe his groin.

Cian grinned, feeling a primitive thrill rush through him. *Huh.*

Peering behind him, Cian twisted a little so he could place his right hand on the sofa cushion. He planted his left foot and heaved. Cian grunted as his muscles strained, but he managed to get his butt onto the sofa.

"Can I help?"

Cian focused on Praerna, a little disappointed to see that his lover already had his loincloth in place. He intended to remove that again soon. There was just something so sexy about the gargoyle's long, purple torso.

"Sure."

While Cian's first impulse was to claim that he was fine, the earnest expression on Praerna's face changed his mind. Holding out his hand, he waited for the small gargoyle to take it. With a surprisingly forceful tug, Praerna helped Cian gain his feet.

"Thanks," Cian stated as he righted his pants and did up his fly. A second later, he took his cane from Praerna. With a smile, Cian repeated, "And thanks."

Praerna beamed at him. "Sure." Then he placed the coffee cake back in the cardboard box and picked it up. Turning back to Cian, he asked, "Are you ready?"

Cian took in the remains of their dinner—or Praerna's breakfast, depending on how a person looked at it.

"Should we clean this up first?" Cian cocked his head as he looked around for some sort of tray.

Shaking his head, Praerna told him, "No. Once we leave, someone will come and take care of it."

While Cian felt a little uncomfortable not cleaning up after himself, he still nodded. "Okay." He waved a hand toward the door. "Are we headed to your room then?" Knowing that was a bit presumptuous, Cian added, "Or would you like to take a walk or . . . something?"

Praerna led the way out of the room. Peering at him from beneath his lashes, he asked, "Would it be forward of me to say that I'd like to head to our suite so we could start our bond?" His voice lowering to a husky rumble, he continued,

"And maybe finish it?"

"*Our* suite?" Cian asked, catching the word choice. Sweeping an appreciative gaze over Praerna, he added in a husky tone, "And I don't mind the sound of that one bit."

Cian watched as a light blush flowed up Praerna's cheeks. "Um, yeah. Our suite." Giving him an earnest look, he added, "If you don't like it, you can redecorate. Or maybe Chieftain Kinsey will let us switch to a different one."

Nodding slowly, Cian told him, "I'm sure it'll be fine." He shrugged, figuring he should have realized that the gargoyles would expect him to move in with Praerna. It was a safety issue, after all. Giving Praerna a reassuring smile, he told him, "I'm not picky."

Praerna grinned up at him, looking a mixture of relieved and pleased.

Cian felt warmth settle in his gut, and his heart thudded a little bit faster upon being on the receiving end of such an adoring look.

Damn, it feels good to please this gargoyle.

Pausing at the bottom of a set of stairs, Praerna glanced at Cian's cane and leg, then met his gaze. "Would you prefer the elevator?"

"What floor are you on?" Cian didn't mind stairs, but the place was huge.

"Third," Praerna told him, nibbling his bottom lip in concern. "The first floor is guest suites and the medical suite," he explained, pointing down the hallways. "Neither are used a whole lot, but it's good to have them." Praerna pointed at the staircase on the right. "That one goes to another wing that houses a few mated couples from before Chieftain Kinsey took over. They're larger, because those people have families or were expected to start them." Snorting, Praerna crossed his arms over his chest. "Although Simon flat-out refused to start a family with Loinad while under Grecian's rule, not that I blame him."

"How about we take the stairs up since we're here," Cian offered, not ready to touch the whole *start a family* thing with a ten-foot pole, yet. "On the way down, you can show me the elevator."

Praerna nodded happily and led the way upstairs.

Cian appreciated that Praerna went slowly and didn't question him about helping. He knew he was slow, but he still had his pride. As they climbed the stairs, they passed a couple of gargoyles heading down, both of the wingless variety. Each time, Praerna introduced Cian as his mate, pride filling his tone, and the cute gargoyle practically glowed with happiness. Both gargoyles greeted Cian with a nod, welcomed him to the clutch, and congratulated them both.

By the time they reached the third floor, Cian felt a bit of a burn in his thigh, and he knew he would need to get off of it soon. He felt a measure of relief when Praerna stopped at the second door on the left. Praerna turned the knob and headed inside.

"Don't lock it?" Cian asked curiously, following.

Praerna shrugged. "Not usually. There's not much to steal, really."

Cian glanced around and saw the truth in Praerna's words. The door had opened into a front room living space. There was a kitchenette to the left with a small round table and four chairs. An open door revealed the corner of a bathroom counter. There was a desk in the living space, and the only object of value rested upon it—a laptop.

While Cian wanted to ask about the lack of personality, he figured the answer would revolve around Chieftain Grecian and his assholeishness.

Don't need to hear about that again.

"I'm gonna put this in the fridge and grab a couple of waters," Praerna told him. He pointed toward the closed door and gave him a shy look. "That's the bedroom. You can go in. I'll be right there."

Cian nodded, smiling at that look, since he'd already seen the pretty gargoyle nude. As he limped into the room, he realized that soon, Praerna would see him naked, too. Sighing, Cian hoped his scarring wouldn't turn off his lover.

He's not the one with a disfigurement. That would be me.

Tossing his soiled shirt toward the closet, Cian settled on the side of the bed. He bent and pulled off his boots and socks. After tucking his socks into the boots, he pushed them toward the foot of the bed, thinking he would need to retrieve his duffel from his motorcycle soon.

Resting his cane against the nightstand, Cian thought about rummaging through it, but he resisted.

"Everything okay?"

Turning his head, Cian peered at Praerna, who was making his way into the room, a bottle of water in each hand.

"It's . . . fine," Cian murmured. With a sigh, he waved toward the scarring on the right side of his torso and admitted his concern. "This is just the beginning, Praerna. It's far worse on my hip and thigh."

"You know I won't care about that," Praerna told him as he set the waters on the nightstand. He pulled open the drawer and reached inside while adding, "Well, I guess that's not totally true." Praerna straightened, surprising Cian by saying, "It's part of who you are. I'll only care insomuch as how it affects your health and movement."

Cian nodded slowly, seeing the belief in Praerna's yellow eyes. Needing to have faith in the gargoyle, he rose to his feet. Undoing his fly once more, Cian hesitated an instant before pushing his jeans and underwear to mid-thigh. He began to bend, intending to take them off, when Praerna rested a hand on his damaged thigh.

"Wait," the gargoyle whispered.

Freezing—more surprised by the touch than responding to his word—Cian straightened.

Praerna smiled up at him as he sank to his knees. "Let me

help."

As Praerna eased his clothes down his legs, Cian sat back on the comforter. "You know, I can do that."

Does Praerna think I'm that handicapped?

"I know." Praerna smiled up at him before refocusing on removing Cian's clothes. "But I like taking care of you. It . . ." He paused to toss the items toward where Cian had left his shirt. Standing, Praerna faced him. "It's in my nature, my instincts, to take care of you. I know you can do things for yourself, but I really like doing things for you, too." Swiping his tongue over his bottom lip, Praerna softly asked, "Does that bother you?"

Cian reached out and took Praerna's hand, threading his fingers with the gargoyle's black claw-tipped ones. "I admit that it'll take some getting used to," he told his lover, squeezing his hand gently. "I'm just not used to it."

Praerna nodded once. "You'll let me know if I go too far or something bothers you?"

Nodding back, Cian promised, "I will." He smiled back at Praerna. "Just as I expect you to do the same. If I do something you don't like, you'll tell me."

Grinning, Praerna stated, "It's a deal."

"Good. Now come up here. I want to explore you," Cian urged, tugging lightly. "Lie down with me."

Praerna climbed up beside him, and Cian released him. He placed his palms on the comforter and scooted backward. Once he was near the middle of the bed, Cian patted the mattress beside him, silently asking Praerna to lie beside him.

Cian rested on his left side and placed his right hand on Praerna's chest. He swept his hand slowly up and down, exploring the firm flesh of his purple gargoyle's abdominals and pecs. The gargoyle's lean torso appeared disproportionally long, and he sported the lines of what looked like a twelve-pack.

The hard hide under Cian's fingers felt so different than his own—lightly ridged, like he imagined a rhino's might be. Still, it was warm and almost seemed to ripple beneath his touch. Cian noted the way Praerna's breathing hitched, his chest heaving.

Pride swelled within Cian upon seeing that response, reveling in the knowledge that Praerna was so affected by his touch.

Noticing Praerna's slender tail where the gargoyle wrapped it around his leg just below his knee, Cian recalled his gargoyle telling him it was sensitive. Curious to find out just how sensitive, he teased the tips of his forefingers along that appendage. The tail twitched, beginning to unwind from its position as Praerna shuddered, gasping softly.

Cian spotted how Praerna's already hardening cock twitched, stretching up from his hairless groin. Humming, Cian narrowed his eyes as he skimmed his fingertips over the tail again, pleased to see the same response. A bead of pre-cum even oozed up from the slit.

The response caused blood to flow to Cian's own prick, and he groaned softly at the pleasure of it.

Meeting Praerna's lust-blown eyes, Cian rumbled, "You like this, don't you, babe?" He gripped Praerna's tail and stroked down it, pulling it from the gargoyle's leg.

In response, Praerna groaned loudly, writhing a little on the bed.

"Oh, damn, Praer," Cian growled, loving that response. "I bet I could get you off like this." He pushed to a sitting position, freeing his left hand, which he quickly wrapped around the sexy gargoyle's purple dick. "Couldn't I?"

"C-Cian," Praerna whined. "Oh, gods!"

"Go ahead, Praerna," Cian encouraged, working both his gargoyle's dick and his tail. "Don't deny yourself. Give in to the pleasure your mate is giving you."

His back bowing, Praerna screamed Cian's name. His cock

pulsed and twitched in Cian's grip. Strands of pearly-white cum burst across the gargoyle's torso, painting his leathery hide.

"Gorgeous," Cian whispered, admiring the view as he eased his ministrations. "Absolutely stunning."

His own cock throbbed at his groin, telling him that he was in a similar state of need.

Releasing Praerna's tail and dick, Cian grabbed the lube from the comforter. He popped the cap and poured a liberal amount onto his fingers, then onto his cock. Cian quickly greased his pole before closing the lube and leaning over Praerna's groin.

Praerna spread his thighs, accommodating him.

Cian peered up at Praerna's face, seeing the heady-lidded, satisfied look there.

"Take me," Praerna encouraged. "I want to feel you inside me."

"Gotta prep you, baby," Cian reminded him. "Never want to hurt you."

When Praerna groaned softly — the sound a desperate whine — Cian chuckled. "Just relax," he encouraged. "I'll take care of you."

Then Cian moved his fingertips to Praerna's entrance. He slipped one finger in deep, the gargoyle opening easily to him. As he worked a second digit in, Cian leaned forward. Sticking out his tongue, he began lapping up Praerna's spend, enjoying the flavor of the gargoyle's lightly salty seed.

Hearing Praerna moan, Cian peered at him through his lashes. He admired his flushed face and the way he panted. Praerna moaned softly, whispering quiet encouragement, expressing his desire for him.

So fucking sexy.

Cian picked up his pace, needing inside his gargoyle almost more than his next breath. The male beneath him was a thing of beauty, all spread out and desperate for him.

"Now, Cian, please now."

Giving in to Praerna's pleas, Cian eased his four fingers from the gargoyle's chute. He rested on his knees, anticipation making it easy to ignore his thigh. Grabbing Praerna's hips, he flipped the small gargoyle.

Praerna eeped in surprise, but when Cian urged him to his knees, he moved swiftly into the position Cian wanted. Gripping the base of Praerna's tail, Cian drew a shocked gasp from the gargoyle. He squeezed lightly, while moving into position behind him. With his free hand, Cian guided his throbbing erection to the gargoyle's hole.

With a rock of his hips, Cian thrust. He groaned when Praerna's muscle immediately gave way, and he found his cock head encased in the hottest, tightest grip of his life. His stomach tightened, and he continued to push, unable to help himself.

With surprising ease, Praerna's passage opened to him.

In seconds, Cian found himself buried balls deep inside the gargoyle. He rocked out halfway, losing himself in the ripple of the muscle caressing his length. His eyes nearly rolled to the back of his head as he did it a second time, then a third.

Heat and pressure set his nerve endings on fire. His balls rolled and tightened in his sack. He forced himself to freeze, fearing he would come embarrassingly fast.

"Don't stop," Praerna immediately urged. He clenched and released his muscles around Cian's embedded prick. "Please, don't stop. Feels so good."

Groaning, Cian gave in to his gargoyle lover's urging. Releasing his lover's tail, he latched both hands onto his hips. Then Cian began to move, slamming into the other man harder than he'd ever done with a lover, moving faster and faster.

Just as Cian had feared, his testicles drew up swiftly. Tingles zipped up his spine, then straight back down to his balls.

Goose bumps broke out along his groin and thighs.

Cian cried Praerna's name as he slammed home one last time, pouring his seed deep inside the gargoyle.

Spots danced across Cian's vision as he experienced the most intense orgasm of his life. Falling forward, he barely caught himself before crushing his lover. Moaning softly, Cian relished their combined scents of male, musk, and seed.

An odd urge struck Cian, and with his face pressed to Praerna's neck, he didn't even hesitate. Instead, he opened his mouth and bit . . . hard.

CHAPTER TEN

Groaning loudly, Praerna arched his back. He flexed his abdominals and his thighs as he eased up and down on Cian's long, thick erection. Tipping his hips, when Praerna eased back down, his human's cock head slid across his prostate just right.

Praerna gasped, his erection twitching in Cian's grip. Looking down, he saw the feral clench of his human's jaw and knew the man was riding a fine edge.

He's close.

Gritting his teeth, Praerna began to trill. At the same time, he clenched his chute muscles. The noise vibrated his body while the constriction intensified the sensations on Cian's erection. Hearing his human bark a cry of obvious shock and delight, Praerna managed to drag himself halfway off his lover's cock one more time before slamming back down again.

Cian roared, the sound music to Praerna's ears. At the same time, his own orgasm slammed into him. Ecstasy rolled through him as he unloaded stream after stream of jizz onto Cian's broad chest.

Groaning and trembling, Praerna flopped forward, sprawling over his large human. He panted softly as aftershocks caused trembles to rack his frame. Praerna muttered his lover's name on a hum.

Feeling hands gliding up and down his back, Praerna smiled. He tipped his chin up and eyed his lover. He loved the sight of Cian panting heavily, his full lips parted as he struggled to take in each breath. Praerna admired his flushed skin, slackened jaw, and the feel of Cian's shaft, slowly softening within his chute.

The prior evening, after their third round, Cian had admitted to him how much he liked being able to cuddle Praerna's body close, keeping his softening prick within him, while they came down from their orgasms. He'd said he'd never experienced anything like it.

Praerna had told him that he loved it, too. He didn't bother sharing that all his prior lovers had been out of his bed before the sheets had cooled. After all, they didn't matter.

Only my mate and his feelings matter.

Well, mine, too, I suppose.

That was something Praerna was still getting used to.

After two days together, building their bond and sharing real-life-time together, Praerna was coming to grips with the fact that even though he was the gargoyle in the relationship, Cian kept assuring him that he wanted to please him just as much.

"Hmmm." Cian rubbed his hands over Praerna's back, tracing along the edges of his wingskins where they attached to his sides. "You somehow feel better every fucking time."

Praerna shivered under the gentle touch to his sensitive appendages. Cian touched him on his wingskins and traced his bone-spurs often. His human had explained that he wanted him to know that he accepted all aspects of him. Praerna loved the reassurance as well as the shivery sensations those touches caused.

"What do you have planned today?" Cian asked softly, slowing his hands' movements to palm his ass.

Feeling Cian's fingertips tease around the base of his tail, Praerna groaned. "So good."

Cian chuckled huskily and moved his hands up his back. "Sorry. Just love touching your differences. They're so fascinating." Obviously thinking along the same track, Cian turned his head and suckled on the point of his ear.

Whining, Praerna shivered under Cian's ministrations. "Y-You're making it h-hard to answer," he muttered.

Chuckling again, Cian skimmed his palms up and down his spine. "I'd apologize, but I know you can scent lies."

Praerna turned his head and rested his chin on the back of one hand. Peering up at Cian, he smiled at him. "I love your touches," he whispered.

"But it won't help us get going with our day," Cian teased with a sexy wink. "So, what do you have planned for the day? Do you have to work?"

Shaking his head, Praerna admitted, "Chieftain Kinsey gives newly mated gargoyles a week off to strengthen their bond, so I don't have to work for another couple of days." He thought about how they'd pretty much spent every waking hour together for the last couple of days—Cian even holding him and easing him through molt—and wondered something else. "I know you were pretty reclusive. Do you, uh . . . do you need some time alone?"

Cian furrowed his brows as he met Praerna's gaze. He hummed a few seconds, his expression turning a little vacant. Cian appeared to be seriously considering his question.

Praerna waited patiently.

A few seconds later, Cian blinked a couple of times. He smiled at Praerna. "Sure, I like my alone time, but that doesn't mean from you. When you go back to work, I'll have more than enough time then." Threading their fingers together, he asked, "Why don't we take a walk in the garden that you and your people are restoring? I'd love to see some of your art. Maybe even watch you tend . . . whatever you'd like."

A sense of warmth flooded Praerna, and he nodded eagerly. "Okay." He hadn't sunk his claws into dirt in days, and he realized that he missed it. Lowering his voice to a husky rumble, Praerna asked, "Can I help you to the shower?"

Cian laughed, his dark eyes full of warmth as he met his gaze. "Sure, but don't think that means you're going to have your wicked way with me." He rolled his hips, jostling his half-hard prick so it slipped from Praerna's body. "You've worn me out, and we've only been up an hour."

Praerna bit back a groan upon feeling Cian's prick slip from his ass. Instead, he waggled his brows as he claimed, "But it was a wonderful hour."

"God, yes," Cian responded huskily, seeming to completely agree with him. "Yes." His expression softened as he rubbed his palms over Praerna's back once more. "I love waking up with you, my gargoyle."

Feeling the heat of a blush trying to steal up his cheeks, Praerna ducked his head. Somehow, Cian's words always affected him like that. They made him feel happiness, warmth, and a little embarrassment all at the same time.

Praerna hoped it never changed.

Half an hour later, Praerna led the way outside, carrying a picnic basket. He squinted up at the blue sky and smiled. Praerna relished being able to walk in the sun with his mate.

Cian walked beside him with a blanket draped over his shoulder. Between Praerna's shorter legs and Cian's slight limp, they had no trouble staying side by side. His human slipped his free arm around Praerna, teasing his fingers along the back of his neck.

Turning his head, Praerna smiled at Cian. "Let's head to the left," he encouraged, pointing. "I did a couple of topiaries near a fountain. I think Welster got the fountain running in the last few days. I heard it was on his *to do* list."

Cian nodded. "Welster. Another gargoyle?"

"Mmm-hmmm," Praerna confirmed. "His hide's a light-brown, and he's one of the winged ones," he explained, knowing Cian was trying to get a handle on everyone who lived there. "Welster's not mated, though, so you may not have seen him around, yet."

Nodding again, Cian asked, "So Welster does plumbing or masonry?"

The sound of the running fountain reached them as they moved through the garden.

"I think Welster could do both," Praerna admitted, leading the way around a trellis covered in climbing roses. "He's sort of the handyman for the clutch."

"I wonder if he needs help with anything," Cian mused. "I'll need something to do after I move here."

Praerna paused, snapping his attention to Cian. "You're moving here?" Hope swelled within him.

Cian cradled Praerna's jaw and smiled down at him. "Of course, I am. This is your clutch, your home." Dipping his head, he pressed a light kiss to Praerna's mouth. "This is where you're safest, with your own kind. I'd never want to put you in jeopardy."

"Thank you," Praerna whispered, butterflies bumping in his belly.

"You're welcome, my gargoyle."

Cian kissed him again, his tongue slipping into Praerna's mouth. Loving the attention, Praerna returned the kiss. He gripped the fabric of Cian's shirt, clutching him close as their tongues dueled.

After a moment, Praerna heard Cian's stomach grumble. They drew back as one, and Cian chuckled softly.

"Let's get that problem taken care of," Praerna teased. After all, he was hungry, too. Ever since he'd molted, his schedule was a little off. Along with all the physical activity — fucking like rabbits was wonderful calisthenics — Praerna found himself hungrier than usual. "We're almost there."

"Sounds good." With a grin, Cian winked. "You helped me work up an appetite earlier."

Praerna eyed his mate, admiring his strong torso and wishing he hadn't bothered with a shirt. "It was my pleasure."

"Mine, too," Cian replied with an eyebrow-waggle.

Happier than he could ever remember being, Praerna couldn't keep the grin from his face as he started walking again.

After one more turn, the fountain appeared. The circular basin had a few cracks in it, but it must have been sound, because it was filled with water. The feature in the center appeared to be a scantily clad woman tipping a jug. Water flowed from it and trickled into a wine goblet held by a reclining male. There was a blanket carved strategically over the man's lap, giving the impression he was nude underneath.

"Huh." Cian cocked his head and eyed the water feature while pulling the blanket from his shoulder. "From what you've said about Grecian, I wouldn't have thought he would commission a piece of art like this."

Praerna shook his head. "He didn't." He placed the basket on a stone bench off to the side. "I heard it was already here when Grecian moved the clutch here over two hundred years ago."

"Then it's old." Cian leaned forward and ran a hand over a crack in the man's thigh. "I bet it could be restored. I'll ask Kinsey if he'd mind if I looked into it."

"I'm sure he'd like that," Praerna stated, taking the blanket from Cian. "Do you want to sit on the blanket or the bench?" he asked as he spread it out next to the bench.

"I'll sit on the blanket with my back to the bench," Cian told him, his attention straying to a bush to the left of it. "That way, I can hold you while we eat." Staring at the bush cut in the shape of a turtle, he commented, "I remember you telling me about this one." Turning to face him, Cian frowned thoughtfully. "I recall you saying you weren't happy with it, but it looks amazing to me."

Praerna smiled at Cian, pleasure filling him upon hearing his words of praise. "Thanks. I fixed it last week."

Cian drew Praerna into his arms, smiling at him warmly. "You're incredibly talented, my gargoyle."

"Thanks," Praerna repeated for lack of anything else to say.

Dipping his head, Cian pressed another kiss to Praerna's lips. He didn't deepen it. Instead, he lifted his head again and smiled at him.

"Your kisses are addictive, Praerna." Cian chuckled ruefully as he eased his hold on him. "I can't seem to get enough of them, but I'm really hungry, too." Moving to the blanket, Cian took Praerna's hand and led him along. "Come on, cutie. Let's sit and eat. This is a beautiful area."

Praerna was more than on board with that. He loved sitting in Cian's arms. He also loved that his human was a cuddler.

As Cian eased onto the blanket, resting his back against the stone bench behind him, Praerna grabbed the basket. He set it on the blanket and knelt next to it. Opening the lid, Praerna began setting everything out.

While Cian had been doing his morning exercises, Praerna had taken the time to make his famous hashbrown casserole. He'd had so many people ask why his tasted slightly different than others — better different. Praerna hadn't told anyone, but he used a zest shredder to scrape green onions, adding the bits in as seasoning.

When Cian had questioned him about it, Praerna had sworn his mate to secrecy.

Praerna placed the dish on the blanket, then pulled out a container with bacon and sausage links. Lastly, he brought out a canister of coffee and one of orange juice. Foregoing plates, Praerna handed Cian a knife and fork.

"Mmmm, that smells delicious," Cian murmured, gripping Praerna's wrist and tugging lightly. "Come here, babe. Let's eat."

Praerna happily went to Cian. His human had his legs spread, so he settled between them. With his side to Cian's chest, he tucked his legs under him and to the side, pressing against the man's strong torso.

Leaning forward, Praerna grabbed the dishes and pulled them close. He stabbed his fork into the hashbrown casserole and scooped out a large bite. It steamed for a few seconds as Praerna brought it to Cian's lips.

"You might want to blow on it," Praerna warned.

Cian did as instructed a couple of times before gingerly taking the bite. As Praerna pulled the fork from his mouth, his mate hummed appreciatively. His eyes closed as he chewed and nodded.

"Oh, that's delicious," Cian told him, praising his skills. "So very good. I see why your friends rave about it."

Beaming a smile at Cian, relief filled Praerna. He was so very glad that his mate liked it. Filling his fork again, Praerna took a bite for himself.

Yup. Delicious.

Cian had just stabbed his own fork into the dish when Simon and Loinad appeared around the hedge.

"I told you I smelled Praerna's hashbrown casserole," Loinad claimed. The pale red gargoyle grinned broadly as both men rushed forward. "Care to share?"

"Pretty, pretty please?" Simon clasped his hands together in front of him and batted his eyelashes. "With sugar on top?"

"Sure." Cian laughed as he held out his fork. "You'll have to share this one. I haven't used it yet."

"Yay!" Simon squealed. Loinad's human mate grabbed the fork and plopped onto the blanket, crossing his legs Indian-style. "Thanks so much."

Loinad settled behind and to the side, his left leg bent and his right one stretched behind Simon. He put his right arm around his mate while reaching for a slice of bacon with his left. Opening his mouth, Loinad accepted a bite of the hash-brown casserole.

"Thanks, babe," Loinad murmured around his mouthful of food. "So good." After he'd swallowed, he smiled. "So, you finally came up for air."

They'd pretty much been holed up in Praerna's quarters for the last three days.

"We did," Cian replied, picking up a piece of sausage with his fingers. "Figured some fresh air would be good."

"Welcome to the clutch," Simon stated before popping a bite of the casserole into his mouth. He moaned softly, which made Loinad chuckle and press a kiss to his neck.

"Thanks for letting us crash your meal." Loinad lifted the bacon to his mouth. Before taking a bite, he asked, "So how are you settling in, Cian? Got any questions we can help with?"

"Doing good," Cian claimed, squeezing Praerna's hip. "Real good." Before biting the sausage link in half, he asked, "Think any of you strong gargoyles can spare your strength and help me move across the country?"

Loinad grinned as he nodded. "That we can do."

CHAPTER ELEVEN

"You're moving in with him?"

Cian heard the incredulity in Tyler's tone, coming through the phone's line, and he could only smile. "Yep," he confirmed. "Praerna's the one."

"You've known him . . . what? Less than a week?"

"Did you get amnesia all of a sudden, Tyler?" Snorting, Cian smirked as he watched Praerna dance and wiggle around in his kitchenette. "I've been talking to him for over six months, remember? Just because I only met him face to face a few days ago doesn't mean shit to me."

"Damn, man." Tyler barked a laugh. "Okay. Okay. What are you gonna do with your place?"

"Sell it," Cian replied, feeling comfortable with his answer. "I don't want to go through the hassle of dealing with renters."

"Wow." Tyler still sounded incredulous. "Well, I'm happy for you. Do I get to meet the guy when you come pack your shit?"

"Of course," Cian assured. "He'll be with me."

"They'll let him leave the commune for however long it takes you to pack up?"

Praerna paused and looked at him, arching one eyebrow ridge.

Cian winked at him, knowing his gargoyle could hear every word Tyler said. He didn't mind that, since he would have shared everything with him anyway. This just saved time.

"I don't plan to take most of the furniture," Cian admitted. "So it shouldn't take long." Relaxing on the sofa, he rested his free arm along the back of it. "Just a couple of heirloom pieces from my father."

"Selling it fully furnished?"

"Yep," Cian confirmed.

Tyler heaved a deep sigh. "Well, you may end up in danger moving in there with him," he warned, sounding disgusted. "The hateful shit this hunter group is spouting is ridiculous times ten." When Cian hesitated to answer, Tyler offered, "Want me to come out there?"

Praerna's eyes widened, looking a little alarmed.

Cian winced. In truth, he wouldn't mind having his buddy closer, but it wasn't his place to alert him to the secret of paranormals. While Cian trusted that Tyler would be able to keep his mouth shut, he'd given his word that he'd never share their existence.

"We both know you're not interested in fighting anymore," Cian reminded his friend. The man had chosen not to re-up as soon as possible after Cian had been medically discharged. "You prefer being behind the scenes, and that's really where I could use you."

"Okay, man, but know that I'd help in a heartbeat."

Smiling, Cian appreciated his buddy's words. The man was damn good with a rifle, but he preferred shooting at paper targets these days. Tyler had even passed up on deer hunting with him the prior year.

"So, anyway. About these hunters," Tyler continued. "From what I've found out, the group has a couple of peeps out your way doing reconnaissance. The leaders are waiting to hear word back about numbers of demons and weaknesses before deciding on the best approach of attack." Tyler's tone turned musing as he continued, "I guess they launched an attack on the place a few months ago, but they never heard back from any of the team. According to these guys, everyone sent disappeared, even the leaders. As it turns out, their old leaders headed it up. Only they knew the exact coordinates, so now those left behind are fixated on this area. They think their leaders were killed, their bodies desecrated in some arcane ritual, and they want payback."

Praerna slapped his hand over his mouth. He wrapped his other arm around his waist, and his body shook with his silent laughter.

"Damn, they actually believe that kind of shit?" Cian found the idea ridiculous, too. "These guys aren't hurting anyone. Just trying to live their life as quietly and happily as possible."

"Yeah, it's shit that people can't just leave people who are different alone." Tyler heaved an annoyed sigh. "I'll keep you posted when I learn a timeframe."

"Thanks, man," Cian replied. "I appreciate it." Before Tyler could hang up, he quickly asked, "Hey, do you know any of these guys' names?"

"Afraid not," Tyler replied, sounding frustrated. "Their encryption is damn good. I haven't been able to figure out who they are or how they're being funded." With a hardness entering his tone, Tyler added, "I'll keep at it, though. Maybe I'll talk to my hacker buddies for ideas."

Grimacing, Cian could see how that could spiral out of control damn fast.

"Better not," Cian countered. "If these hunters are as crazy as you say, there's no telling what they could decide to do with people who they think are collaborating with these demon worshippers." Thinking quickly, Cian added, "And it may be stereotyping, but most hackers aren't as able to defend themselves like you can."

"You're probably right," Tyler agreed. "Better not add targets to these weirdos' lists." The sound of a pan being placed on the stove clanged through the line. "Okay. Talk to you later, Huntsman. Stay safe. Call if you need anything."

"Will do," Cian responded.

Then Tyler disconnected the line.

"There always seems to be more hunters, no matter how many we deal with." Praerna settled on the sofa beside Cian and held out a plate to him. "Until people learn how to accept people who are different, they'll just keep coming back."

Cian took the slice of coffee cake after setting his phone on the side table. "Considering human nature, I don't see that happening any time soon."

"No," Praerna murmured with a sigh. Then he took a bite of the coffee cake and hummed, his mind clearly going to the delicious food.

Seeing as Cian had nothing to report to Kinsey from Tyler's call, he allowed himself to be distracted by the tasty treat, too.

"You ready for your first motorcycle ride?" Cian asked, holding his helmet out to his gargoyle, who currently wore his human skin.

"Don't you need that?" Praerna asked, staring at the helmet dubiously.

"We'll head to town and buy a second one," Cian assured, waggling the item.

Praerna lifted his hands, palms out. "You should wear it," he insisted. "Sure, I may look human, but I'm really not." Then he pointed at his spikey hairdo. "Plus, it'd ruin my hair."

"You're in Wyoming," a deep voice stated. "Helmets aren't mandatory for adults in this state."

Cian turned to see Enforcer Biers in human form, wheeling a motorcycle toward them. Beside him, doing the same, was his lion shifter mate, Dyson. Neither wore a helmet, although both had on leather jackets and motorcycle boots.

"Huh. Didn't realize that," Cian admitted, placing the helmet on his own head. He scowled as he eyed Praerna. "Still think we should get you one."

Praerna smiled brightly, reaching up to work the clasp of Cian's helmet. "Okay." Sliding his fingertips along Cian's jaw, he told him, "If that's what you want, but I feel so much better seeing the helmet on you, my human."

Nodding, Cian told him, "The law or not, safety first."

"Exactly." Praerna nodded back. Then he glanced between Biers and Dyson. "You guys going to town, too? Or just out exploring?"

"We're going with you," Dyson told him, slinging his leg over his *Harley*. "Hunters are about. No one goes anywhere alone."

Biers nodded. "Exactly."

"Oh, damn," Cian muttered, wincing. "I didn't think of that." Meeting Praerna's gaze, he offered, "Maybe we should plan our outing after the hunters are dealt with."

Praerna quickly shook his head. "We are not putting our lives on hold because of them." Then he shrugged and added, "Besides, there will always be the threat of hunters. The only way to avoid that would be to move the clutch, and we'd only do that as a last resort."

"Yep, moving the clutch is damn difficult," Biers explained, getting on his own motorcycle. "There are only so many secluded places left in the world."

Cian swung his right leg over his *Honda* before tucking his cane into his custom-made holder. "Yeah, humans do like to breed like rabbits." He held his hand out to Praerna. "Shall we?"

Praerna grinned and nodded eagerly. He took Cian's hand and carefully swung up behind him. Praerna wrapped his arms around Cian's waist, cuddling close to his back.

"Is this okay?" Praerna asked. "Will it be too hard with

your thigh?"

Cian understood why Praerna asked. Although he didn't like his smaller lover thinking of him as weak, it was a fact of life. His leg would never be good as new, even after bonding with his gargoyle.

"It'll be fine," Cian assured. "It's why I had you mount while still using the kickstand," he explained. "It's holding our weight. Once we get started, it won't even be an issue. We'll just need to be a little careful when mounting and dismounting."

Catching Praerna's nod out of the corner of his eye, Cian fired up his motorcycle. "Thanks for coming with us, guys," he offered as he heard Biers and Dyson do the same.

"Happy to get out," Dyson told him, a grin creasing his full lips. "We enjoy riding, too, but life keeps us busy here so much." With a wink at Biers, he added, "But this, we're doing our duty and having fun."

Easing off the kickstand, Cian righted his motorcycle. He started them moving, relieved that the gargoyles' road was paved. While he could ride on gravel, it was a pain in the ass. Plus, Cian had to relearn balance due to having someone behind him.

"Does your motorcycle helmet have a microphone?" Biers asked, flanking him on the right.

Dyson took position a bit behind them.

"It does," Cian replied. "I ride with Tyler on occasion, and it's nice to be able to communicate."

"I hear those are pretty nice," Dyson called with a laugh. "Good thing we have paranormal hearing and can holler over the roar of the wind."

Laughter was exchanged as they turned onto the road.

"So where are we going?" Biers asked.

"I don't really know the roads around here," Cian admitted. "I was just going to wander." Glancing Biers' way, he asked, "Got any good recommendations?"

"Let's take them to Thompson Falls," Dyson piped up. "It's about an hour away with a short hike over pretty level ground. It'll give us a chance to stretch our legs before heading into Lake Point for a bite to eat."

"You just want to stop at that café that has the potato salad you like," Biers teased, chuckling deeply.

"Well, their sign is right. They have the best potato salad in Lake Point," Dyson replied, completely unabashed. "Plus, their meatball sub is damn good . . . and huge."

"Sounds like a plan," Cian replied with a laugh. "I'll follow you guys."

For the next hour, Cian did just that. Biers took the lead, Cian kept to the middle, and Dyson followed. They chatted a little, and Cian discovered he liked the pair.

Dyson was the friendlier of the two, while Biers was quieter. The gargoyle had been an enforcer for just over a decade before the clutch had been taken over by Grecian. He'd already been mated, and when the change had happened, he'd done his duty. As much as Biers hadn't agreed with Grecian's changes, he hadn't been powerful enough to stop them.

Biers had been damn grateful to see Kinsey take over.

"You about ready for that hike?" Biers asked, turning into a lane that sported a sign for the falls. "And did anyone think to bring water?"

"I did, handsome," Dyson assured with a grin. "I brought one for all of us."

"You're the man, my mate," Biers replied, flashing a smile his lover's way.

"Yup," Dyson replied with a laugh.

Cian chuckled softly as Praerna snickered.

Entering the parking lot, Cian saw several vehicles already parked there. He recognized one as the *Jeep* that had been at the bed and breakfast. As Cian parked several spaces away from the nearest vehicle—Biers and Dyson easing in next to him—he tried to remember their names, but he was drawing a blank.

Oh well. Doubt they'd recognize me anyway.

"Be careful," Cian urged, holding his left hand out and up to offer Praerna support while dismounting.

"It's beautiful out here," Praerna stated a little breathlessly as he took Cian's hand and swung off the bike. Pitching his voice low, he murmured, "I know I've lived here for nearly two hundred years, but I've never had the opportunity to see much of the area."

"I'm glad I'm able to help you change that," Cian replied. Taking off the helmet and placing it on a handlebar, he enjoyed Praerna's wide-eyed look as he peered around the trailhead. In fact, Cian liked it so much that he decided he needed a taste of it. "Come'ere."

Cian gripped Praerna's wrist and tugged. With a giggle, Praerna came, resting his thigh against Cian's since he still straddled the bike.

That didn't stop Cian from claiming Praerna's lips in a short, hot liplock.

Dyson's deep chuckle reminded Cian that they couldn't get carried away. After all, the place was public. Cian had no desire to scandalize anyone.

Drawing the kiss to an end, Cian grinned at Praerna. His lips were just a little kiss-swollen, and Cian loved that look on his lover. While Cian missed Praerna's pretty purple skin, there were advantages to seeing him in his human form, too.

After Cian eased off his motorcycle, he grabbed his cane. He took a few limping steps to relax his thigh, stretching the muscle and warming it in preparation for a stroll. Then Cian locked up his helmet and their jackets before taking the water from Dyson and heading toward the trailhead.

They stopped long enough for Praerna to read the sign before they headed onward again.

CHAPTER TWELVE

Praerna clung to Cian's back, enjoying the breeze on his face. The flavor of the potato salad served at the café still clung to his taste buds. Just as Dyson had claimed, it had been fantastic.

I wonder if I can recreate it.

Praerna figured he would probably have to eat it a few more times to do that . . . not that doing so would be a hardship. There were several more sandwiches he would like to try, even though his roast beef and Swiss sub had been amazing. The place had a great menu.

"Did you enjoy your first dining out experience?" Cian asked, turning his head to half-peer back at him.

"Definitely," Praerna replied, squeezing Cian's waist. "They had great food."

"Told you their potato salad was the best," Dyson stated, grinning at them. "They bake their own bread, too."

"Is that why it was warm?" Praerna wondered.

"Maybe," Biers replied, shrugging his massive shoulders. "But most likely it was because they heated it to melt the Swiss cheese before serving it." The gargoyle enforcer continued to explain, saying, "Some of their sandwiches are cold."

"Oooohh," Praerna mused, nodding. "That makes sense."

Cian glanced toward the pair traveling with them and asked, "Are there other restaurants in Lake Point?"

"If you want fine dining for a nice date or something, you'll have to go farther out," Dyson told him, grinning as if reading his mind. "Everything around here is a little more rustic."

"What about that barbeque place?" Biers sounded a little offended. "That place is a great date place."

Dyson laughed, grinning at his mate. "Yes, it is, my mate. It's a perfect date place for guys like us." With a wink, he added, "Other guys just might be interested in something a little more . . . upscale."

"Don't know why," Biers grumbled.

Chuckling, Cian told them, "We'd be happy to check out the barbeque place sometime." He reached back and squeezed Praerna's knee. "Right, babe?"

"Absolutely!" Praerna laughed. "I'm willing to try just about anything." Sweeping his arm to indicate the area, he stated enthusiastically, "Getting to go out anywhere is amazing!"

"We'll do it again soon," Cian assured him, squeezing his knee again before returning his hand to the handlebar.

The roar of an engine coming up behind them caught Praerna's attention. Turning his head, he spotted a *Jeep* gaining on them. The engine grew louder as it swiftly closed the distance between them.

Praerna saw Cian look in his rearview mirror, his lips turning down into a frown. "What the hell?" he grumbled when the *Jeep* drew close to their motorcycles, then backed off again, only to draw close again and honk.

"What assholes," Biers grumbled loudly.

"Some people just don't like motorcyclists," Dyson commented, sounding annoyed. "What do you want to do?"

Before Biers could reply, the *Jeep* pulled up next to them. "You said you were just passing through, Cian." A blonde woman hollered from the passenger side. She scowled at him and lifted her arm, revealing a handgun. "And now I see you out with monsters. You really should have kept going."

Cian slammed on the brakes just as the sound of a gunshot echoed through the forest.

"Son of a bitch," Biers roared while veering closer to the *Jeep*. He started to reach for the gun, since the woman was swinging it to aim at Cian again.

Obviously seeing the move, the driver yanked the wheel, veering the *Jeep* sharply toward Biers.

Biers roared and gunned his *Harley*, shooting forward and out of danger . . . for the second.

Cian weaved back and forth behind the *Jeep* as the woman took shot after shot at him, all the while screaming profanities and yelling about how he'd chosen the wrong side.

Two things happened nearly at the same time.

Biers leaped from his motorcycle, launching himself straight into the air. As he shifted to his true form, his wings and larger frame rent the clothes from his upper body. He dipped a black wing and swooped toward the *Jeep*.

Just as Biers attempted to land in the back of the vehicle, a gunshot came from behind them. The *Jeep* lurched to the left, the rear right tire blowing. The driver began cussing a blue streak as he battled to keep the vehicle on the road while speeding up in an attempt to avoid Biers landing in the back of the open-topped vehicle.

As the woman screamed, firing at Biers nearly point-blank, Praerna tried to look behind them. Fear worked through him. He tensed, waiting for another shot from behind them.

"What the hell have you gotten into, Cian?" A voice that Praerna vaguely recognized came through Cian's helmet speaker.

"Tyler?" Cian looked to the right as a man on another motorcycle appeared next to them. "What the hell are you doing here?"

"Watching your back, buddy," Tyler replied. He held some sort of gun in his right hand and pointed it toward the *Jeep* . . . or Biers. "Been here since the day after you arrived. Didn't like the hunter chatter about this place. Was worried." Lifting his gun, Tyler pointed at Biers. "You said there weren't any demons, man. What the fuck?"

"Don't shoot Biers," Cian ordered, shaking his head. "And that's a gargoyle, not a demon."

"A gargoyle?" Tyler gaped at him for a few seconds. "Those things are *real*?"

"Yep, they're real." Dyson joined them, riding on Tyler's other side. "Who's your friend, Cian?"

"This is Tyler." Cian waved his hand between them. "Tyler, that's Dyson." He used a thumb to point over his shoulder. "My man, Praerna. Those assholes must be part of the hunter reconnaissance team you mentioned, Tyler. They're trying to fuck up the end of our date."

"Although how they realized we aren't human, I don't know," Dyson cut in with a growl.

"We'll have to ask them," Praerna muttered, uncertainty filling him. "Why aren't we helping Biers?"

Dyson laughed. "He considers this having fun." Then he snorted while shrugging. "And he'd yell at me for putting myself in danger."

As they'd been talking, Praerna had seen Biers slam the head of the blonde woman against one of the *Jeep's* roll bars, causing her to slump in her seat. The driver had yanked a gun from somewhere. Before he'd even managed to get off a shot, Biers grabbed the guy's wrist. He must have squeezed, for the man screamed and dropped the weapon.

When Biers released him, the man began swerving back and forth, clearly trying to shake Biers free of the vehicle. Unfortunately, with the blown tire, he quickly lost control. The *Jeep* hit the soft berm. The tire sank, and the vehicle veered wildly, slamming headfirst into a tree.

The driver must not have been wearing a seatbelt, for he flew forward right through the windshield. His head hit the tree, and he collapsed on the hood of the vehicle, his neck at an odd angle. Biers had managed to grab the woman and jump clear, and he floated to the ground.

Turning, Biers raked his gaze over the area. He stopped at them, looking at Tyler for just a second. Then he pinned his attention on Dyson as he stalked toward him.

"You okay, my mate?" Biers asked gruffly. Switching his hold to carry the woman with one hand, he cupped Dyson's neck. "Were you hit?"

"I'm just fine, my mate," Dyson replied, resting his hand on Biers' chest. His expression turned rueful as he stared at Biers. "The same can't be said of you. How many times did she get you?"

"Just twice, but they barely penetrated," Biers stated dismissively. "They weren't really set up for taking down a gargoyle."

"They were going hiking the morning I came to you with Tyler's information," Cian stated, turning off his motorcycle engine. "They must have been part of the reconnaissance in the area."

Biers nodded. "Makes sense." He peered back down the road. "Any idea what happened to my bike?"

Dyson chuckled. "It hit a tree, my mate."

"Damn it," Biers grumbled. "That'll be an expensive fix."

"Uh, you guys are acting really lackadaisical about just being in a firefight while riding your bikes," Tyler stated, staring at them in confusion. "Doesn't this concern you?" He pointed at Biers. "What if someone sees you? I mean, other than me. Obviously, this is a big damn secret."

"We'll take you to Chieftain Kinsey, Tyler," Dyson stated, smirking at the human. "You'll have to be sworn to secrecy, too, but he'll want to thank you for your help."

"O-Okay," Tyler muttered, although he didn't sound too sure or okay with that news.

Cian must have realized it, too. He reached over and patted

Tyler's shoulder. "It's fine, Tyler," he told him. "I promise. No harm will come to you." With a scoff, Cian added, "You've just entered a much bigger world."

"Swell," Tyler muttered, holstering the gun he'd still been holding. "And if you're going to run the risk of facing down hunters while driving down the street, you need to start going everywhere armed."

Nodding, Cian smiled at his friend. "You're absolutely right."

"Damn straight, I am," Tyler grumbled.

"I've called it in to Second Destrawn," Biers announced, lowering his phone and shoving it back into his jeans. "I'm going to get this woman to the estate." He focused on Dyson. "You'll escort them?"

"Of course," Dyson replied. After accepting a kiss from the gargoyle, he added, "Be careful, and see you soon."

Biers nodded. "Same to you." Then the gargoyle spread his wings, bent his knees, and leaped into the air.

In seconds, Biers had disappeared between the trees, using them for cover.

"Let's get going, then," Dyson ordered, firing up his motorcycle once more.

Cian and Tyler followed suit.

"Are you all just going to leave it like this?" Tyler waved a hand to indicate the wrecked vehicle and the dead driver.

Dyson shook his head. "A clean-up crew is on the way. They're trained to handle these sorts of things," he told him. Then Dyson grinned wickedly. "Plus, they'll have a vampire with them, so they'll be able to alter minds."

"Vampire?"

Praerna barely heard Tyler whisper the word, only due to his sensitive paranormal hearing.

"Yep." Cian patted Tyler on the shoulder again. "Don't worry. There'll be plenty more shocks. Come on."

Then Cian started them moving. As he drove, he reached back and squeezed Praerna's knee. "Are you okay, my gargoyle? Were you injured?"

"I'm okay," Praerna assured, hugging him tightly. "You kept us safe."

Cian peered over his shoulder at him. "Always, my gargoyle. Always."

Praerna knew a vow when he heard one. While he might be the paranormal in the relationship, Cian lived up to his name — Huntsman. His mate was his protector.

As Praerna realized that, he decided he was okay with it. After all, the paranormal didn't always have to be the one in charge.

And when we get home and things get settled, I'll shower my mate with love and show him how much I appreciate him.

Looking forward to that, Praerna held on tight as Cian drove them home.

ABOUT THE AUTHOR

Charlie started writing fantasy when she was eight, and after stumbling onto her first erotic romance at age nineteen, she realized her true calling. She now focuses on writing gay erotic romance, normally of the paranormal variety, with heroes of all kinds. With the help and support of her husband, Charlie finally fulfilled one of her life-long goals . . . move to acreage with her horses. You can often find her curled up with her laptop and a cup of tea or glass of wine, creating her next adventure. Charlie enjoys exploring the mountains of her new Oregon home on horseback, 4-wheeler, or motorcycle.

She can be reached at ch.richards2010@yahoo.com

Or visit her at www.charlie-richards.com.

www.ingramcontent.com/pod-product-compliance
Lightning Source LLC
Chambersburg PA
CBHW071128130626
46555CB00016B/1044